# CHAR

# CHARLIE'S WAR

### KEVIN DOHERTY

TCMG Books

First published in 2016 by Endeavour Press
as a Kindle ebook
This edition published in 2016 by TCMG*

Front cover design Endeavour Press

ISBN 978-1541090668

A CIP catalogue record for this book is available from
the British Library.

*The Corporate Marketing Group Limited Registered No. 2652455 England
Registered office: Knoll House, Knoll Road, Camberley GU15 3SY

For Ben, Liam and Sean, with love

# 1

Early on that sleepy August afternoon in 1941, Charlie Quinn took off in his Spitfire from RAF Hawkinge in Kent and crossed into the English Channel at Folkestone, where the strollers on Marine Parade, the young lovers and the families enjoying a blessed sunny respite from war, paused and shielded their eyes to gaze up as he headed towards German-occupied France.

As he climbed to operating height he glanced around to check that his wingman Tim Kemp, in an identical Spitfire, was holding position off his right wing and slightly behind him. Kemp's job was to watch for enemy aircraft trying to blindside them from behind or below, a danger not only once they reached German-held territory but also over the Channel itself.

Satisfied that Kemp was in place and all was as it should be, Charlie continued on a south-easterly bearing, reaching the French shore near the green cliffs and crumbling rocks of Équihen with its cluster of fishermen's cottages, south of the port of Boulogne. This kept them clear of the German anti-aircraft guns that defended the port. From Équihen he swung south to follow the long, gentle curve of the coast. It was a circuit he and Kemp had followed many times.

On this particular day the weather over north-western France was even more glorious than that in

England – endless blue sky with only light drifts of cirrocumulus at twenty thousand feet. Nothing else marred that clear sky, its purest azure bleaching almost to white where it washed down to the horizon. This was the Côte d'Opale – the Opal Coast, beloved of artists and painters – and today its crystal-clear light and the colours it drew from the landscape and ocean were living up to its name.

Charlie's heart ached at the beauty of it. Fishing villages and small lakes passed below his wings. It was a coastline and region he knew well. In happier times – before this war, before the Germans came, before they ruined things – this would have been a day for exploring the pine forests, a day for dallying beside any of the scores of little streams that veined and watered the land, a day for dozing among the sand dunes with the only sound the rustle of the high grasses and whisper of the surf. A day for lazy kisses. A day for falling in love. For falling in love with Émilie.

'Don't be cruel to me, Charlie,' she had chided on that other sunny afternoon as they lay together on the glittering sand. Before the war; before the Germans.

*Sharr-lee.* He loved how she said his name. But then, he loved everything about Émilie.

He raised himself on an elbow and let a handful of warm sand trickle through his fingers.

'I'm not being cruel, Émilie, I'm being practical. There's a war coming. I have to go back to England.'

'You're leaving me.' She turned away from him. He watched the light shimmering in the blonde streaks that the summer had brought to her hair.

'Not if you come with me,' he said.

'But France is my home.'

'England can be your home.'

The blonde tresses shook. 'Nonsense, Charlie. How can that be?'

'If you marry me.'

It was war that was cruel. War had come, just as he said it would, even though war was supposed never to be possible again, and it changed everything, even the meaning of sunshine and clear skies. Now this beautiful day was a day not for love but for hunting Germans. For killing them. Or being killed by them. It was a day for sweeping the coast down to the western tip of Picardy and back again, for luring Messerschmitts – the yellow-nosed Bf 109s that infested the region – from their base at Abbeville and blowing them from the skies. Hitler's airborne war machine had taken heavy losses a year ago in what Churchill had called the Battle of Britain, the battle that was Charlie's blooding, the battle that had made him a hero – a term he dismissed: there were no heroes, there were only those who managed to remain alive – but the Luftwaffe was still a force to be reckoned with and had to be kept in check.

'Look at it the way a farmer thinks of vermin,' Henry Banham liked to say. Banham was Charlie's CO at Hawkinge. 'Regular culling, that's the only way to prevent the filthy creatures overrunning everything. Europe's lost. Adolf has the whole damned lot in his fist, or as much of it as matters. We're the only ones left. The Germans won't stop of their own accord, there'll always be more of them, they'll just keep coming. Fact of life. So we cull.' A scything motion with his hand to drive the point home. 'Again. And again.' The motion being repeated each time. 'As often as it takes. There simply is no other way. Keep up the pressure. You're my best pilot, Charlie, best of breed – I'm counting on you.'

So this was Charlie's work. Young man's work, with Charlie, at twenty-four, already one of the oldest, the most experienced. Charlie the hero, the ace, this was what he had to do. For Émilie. For their child as well now – a son born on the first day of that fearsome air battle. And for the memory of Charlie's father. Always for him. Never spoken of but never far from his thoughts.

The coast was quiet, no 109s in sight. Not even any German trucks or other vehicles on the coastal roads when he descended for a quick check.

He climbed back up, looping out over the sea to turn, and headed north again. Over his shoulder he saw that Kemp was still in position. Far below them and to their right lay Le Touquet, its promenades and broad boulevards and web of streets once the haunt of the wealthy, of the well-heeled English as much as the French. The occupation would have turned its elegant villas into German billets by now. Down there too was the wide bay of the Canche. Low tide, with little boats marooned on the sandbar, mere specks against the dun sand.

And where the Canche narrowed, he knew without looking, across the bridge was the small village of Étaples. Not fashionable, not elegant, little Étaples. An ordinary place, for ordinary people.

Étaples. The name sent a shudder through him.

'Someone stepping on your grave,' Kemp would have said had he seen the shudder. A man of endless superstitions was Tim Kemp. Wore his shirt inside out on sorties and carried a St Christopher medallion on every flight. Superstitious and religious, which Charlie, being neither, considered one and the same.

'Not my grave,' he could have told Kemp. 'The grave's not mine.'

Could have told him but would not have done. Would not have said whose grave. Would only have smiled as he always did at Kemp's eccentric notions, clapped him on the shoulder and sipped beer with him in The Cat and Custard Pot down the lane in Paddlesworth – but said not a word.

The land below was becoming marsh and scrubland. The Channel was still as calm and smooth as if painted on glass and the skies all around were still empty. Today, it seemed, the enemy was lying low. No yellow-nosed rats were stirring, nothing troubled the idyllic expanse of sky as he scanned around. Even the thin drifts of cloud were melting away. The mission was beginning to feel like a leisurely drive on a Sunday afternoon. He glanced over at Kemp as the other Spitfire drew briefly alongside. Observing the radio silence that Charlie always stipulated, Kemp shook his head slowly – nothing doing, the gesture said.

Charlie pondered. Still plenty of fuel in the tanks. Shame to come all this way for nothing. Abbeville, though behind them, was only a few minutes away. Maybe they should double back and venture inland, catch the rats in their nest. Quick in and out, and with any luck strafe a clutch of aircraft on the ground before anyone knew what was happening. There were said to be as many as fifty fighters based there; could be sitting ducks.

On the other hand, they might raise more 109s than they could cope with. A patrol of three or four here along the coast was one thing, better still a sortie on its way to England; that was the kind of target they had come looking for – 'Regular culling, Charlie, the only way' – but a reception committee of a dozen would be another matter.

He glanced again at Kemp, who raised a gauntleted hand in a shrug, his thoughts evidently much the same as his own. Then Kemp inclined his head towards him: your decision, the nod said.

But it was a decision that was never made.

## 2

Earlier that day, Charlie's commanding officer, Henry Banham, a man as thin as a reed – 'Because you're such a worrier, dear,' his wife Rosemary was forever telling him – drove to central London on a mission of his own. A discreet mission. Walls had ears, the public information posters warned. Henry agreed. And RAF switchboards had ears too; hence his decision to come to the capital in person. He had even dressed not in his usual RAF blue-grey but in a plain civilian suit and wide-brimmed fedora – the latter an unseasonal choice given the hot weather but considered essential to anonymity by Henry. 'Too many American films, dear,' Rosemary would have told him.

No sooner had he arrived in Marylebone than it occurred to him that streets could be as treacherous as walls and switchboards, for streets had eyes, especially if the street in question was synonymous with one particular profession; being seen there could give rise to all sorts of questions he did not care to answer. So Henry decided that he most certainly did not want to park in the telltale street where he had an appointment. He even removed the RAF Hawkinge permit from his windscreen.

Such a worrier, Henry Banham.

So now here he was, weaving his way through Marylebone, his shirt sticking to his thin back in the

August heat and his parched throat crying out for a decent cup of tea.

Parking took a while. The so-called Blitz that Hitler had unleashed on Britain's cities had hit London hard; even now, months later, the work of demolition and clearance and making safe was still going on. Every street seemed to be clogged by piles of rubble and teams of workmen. The noise was horrendous – a cacophony of sledgehammering, shovelling, shouting, clattering. There was also the smell to contend with, a halitosis of dead air that had been held captive for decades in old walls and timbers and basements, an exhalation that would have been foul enough on its own even without the odours from broken sewer pipes.

At last Henry found a spot in a side street off Marylebone Road and walked back to his destination. This was Harley Street, home of the world's finest physicians, surgeons and practitioners of every medical specialism. Prime ministers and royalty came here. But even privileged Harley Street had not been spared by the Luftwaffe's bombers. Entire terraces of its handsome buildings were gone; deep craters and wreckage scarred many of the rest.

Henry counted his way to the correct doorway in a miraculously untouched block, rang the bell beside its brass plate – as brightly polished as any statement of defiance could possibly be – and announced himself as plain Mr Banham. He took a quick look around in search of the prying eyes he had taken such lengths to avoid, then whipped off the fedora and stepped smartly inside.

'Henry, old chap,' said the distinguished doctor into

whose consulting rooms he was ushered a minute later. 'How long has it been?'

The man was a trusted friend, someone Henry had known since their days at university. He was also one of the most experienced and respected men in his field, which was why he could afford to install himself in Harley Street. Just as important, he did not work for the War Office, the Air Ministry, the Royal Air Force or any other official body to which he might owe fealty. He would keep his mouth shut. He would keep Henry's little secret.

The two men spent a few minutes in small talk and reminiscences. To Henry's relief, a pot of tea arrived and the honours were done.

Then the doctor lit a cigarette. His expression became stern.

'I've studied all the test results, Henry. I'm confident I now have all the information I need.'

Furrows creased Henry's bony forehead. 'To make a diagnosis.'

The doctor nodded. 'Not good news, Henry. In a nutshell, I'm afraid I concur with your own suspicions.'

'Oh dear. I feared as much. Hoped you wouldn't but feared you might. So I have a bit of a problem, do I?'

'You do, yes. Sorry, old chap.'

'Better spell it out for me, then.'

Henry set down his cup and saucer and listened closely to what his eminent friend had to say.


In north-western France, a doctor of a very different kind and whose vocation was in a setting quite unlike

London's Harley Street – though a feature in common was provided by the heavy aroma that drifted through the hot afternoon air from a nearby septic tank – mopped sweat from his face and neck, fitted his bicycle clips around his ankles and ensured that his medical bag was firmly secured to his bicycle's pannier. He thrust two fingers between his lips and whistled to call his dog from its investigations in the depths of the nearby woodland, part of the ancient Forest of Hardelot.

This doctor was called Philippe Destry. He was thirty-four years old, unexceptional in terms of height and build but set apart from other men by the magnificence of his Gallic nose, a noble feature. Except for a rim of light-brown hair around the sides and back of his head, he was bald, which he regretted. But on the other hand, he was unmarried, having resisted the many female admirers over the years who had fallen for his gentle character and amber eyes, and this bachelorhood was a condition in which he rejoiced. He was the only doctor in the small rural commune of Auny-sous-Bois, which lay by the forest and between Hardelot and Boulogne. He never charged his patients enough, in fact never charged many of them at all, but somehow he got by.

Philippe had experienced only two significant periods of unhappiness in his life. The first was his years of study in Paris, which, although the studies themselves enthused him, had kept him from his much-loved Auny-sous-Bois for far too long. The second was this time of war in which he now found himself.

These interferences aside, he was by and large an optimistic sort of man. But there were limits. Today was an example. As his dog Eiffel – a small white terrier of uncertain lineage and with a permanently bent right ear – bounded over to stand panting beside him, Philippe sighed and turned for a final word with the patient he had just been visiting.

This man lumbered flat-footedly from his cottage to see him off, puffing with each pace, his arms dangling loosely as if to balance his belly. In truth the belly was only a modest protuberance now, a shadow of what it had been before these days of German requisitions and rationing, but the man's distinctive gait had become a fixed part of him and still conjured the impression of a ship labouring through heavy seas.

'Bernard, you drink too much and you don't look after yourself,' Philippe chastised him. He gestured at the pieces of cars and vans and agricultural machinery that crammed the large yard surrounding Bernard's home, which was also his business premises – Auny's one and only repair garage. 'You're a good garagiste, you work hard at these hopeless old crocks, but it's not good for you. I know things have been difficult since your wife died and with your son away, and I know you need to take your mind off things, but your only exercise is wielding a screwdriver or spanner. Your heart can't take it. Keep this up and you'll be dead in a couple of years. I tell you the same thing over and over, which you must surely find tedious. Write down my words and recite them to yourself next time you think you need me. It'll save us both a lot of effort.' Philippe wrinkled his nose. 'And do something about that septic tank. The gases from that alone could finish you off.'

The garage owner released a wheezy chuckle. His breath stank of alcohol. 'Listen, my friend, the way things are we'll all be dead soon enough. We've only had a year of Boche jackboots on our throats so far – the worst is yet to come. So I enjoy myself while I can. Why shouldn't a lonely widower do that? You're a single man, you might understand if you weren't so self-righteous. What pleasure do I have other than the occasional sip of wine or beer? And as for these old crocks, they're a pleasure too and not hopeless to me. They provide components, tyres, batteries – every garage's lifeblood, especially these days. Nothing is wasted.'

'Where's the point – who can get petrol these days?'

'Where there's a will, there's a way.'

Philippe tutted. 'You mean your black market friends.'

'There you go again – all high and mighty. I'm just being helpful. I could set you up with a good little car and put you in touch with someone who'd get you petrol coupons – save you all that cycling.'

'I don't mind cycling. And I don't break the law.'

Bernard rolled his eyes. 'Where are you off to now – another patient to torture?'

'A social call on my brother. Any news of your son, by the way?'

The garage owner's florid face darkened. The weight he had lost made his skin loose, as if it was too large for him. His jowls wobbled as he shook his head.

'No letter, Philippe – the Germans don't let him

write.' Bernard dropped his voice to a whisper. A furtive gleam crept into his eyes. 'Things are beginning to move, you know. That's what I hear.'

'Are you still speaking of your son?'

'No. Obviously.'

'Well, you're talking in riddles.'

'I'm being careful.'

'In case the trees are listening?'

'Be serious, Philippe. In Paris and other big cities people are starting to come together, make plans, organise themselves. At last, thank God. Ordinary citizens like you and me. They're calling it resistance, Philippe, a resistance movement – and it's growing.'

Philippe looked unconvinced. 'Ordinary citizens? Stupid youngsters, you mean, with silly underground pamphlets no better than student newspapers. That's what you're talking about. Children with no sense.'

'You'd hardly call the miners senseless children. They're out on strike.'

'Just what we need. So we'll have no coal at all this winter. There's little enough since it's been rationed.'

'And who rationed it, Philippe? Ha! Anyway, the Boche won't have any either, to power their armament factories, and that's what matters. You know, I wouldn't wonder if we see assassinations as resistance grows. Why not? Mow the Boche down in our streets. No city boulevard or country lane safe for them.' He mimed using a machine gun, spraying bullets from side to side and making what he considered suitable noises.

'Do you have any idea how foolish you look, Bernard? You're getting yourself overexcited. Your heart will give out. And what will this heroic resistance achieve?'

'Send the Boche packing.'

Philippe laughed. 'Really? Where on earth do you hear these tales?'

'Now that Hitler's turned on Stalin and marched into Russia, our communists have woken up. They've formed themselves into a single national group. A shrewd move – gives them real muscle.'

'Since when have French communists ever agreed on anything? Besides, muscle to do what?'

'We need freedom fighters. You know – like the francs-tireurs of old, when it was us against the Prussians.'

'You're a dreamer, Bernard. It's a very nice quality, I suppose.'

'And you've become a cynic, Philippe.'

'Incidentally, they're not Boche. They're Germans. You should be more respectful.'

'They're Nazis.'

'National Socialists, Bernard.'

'They've no right to be here. This is our country.'

'Of course it is. And the Germans agree. Our own Marshal Pétain agrees. Now there's a real hero for you. It's thanks to him that we're still allowed our own government.'

Bernard snorted and spat on the ground. Eiffel jumped back in alarm.

'Call that a government and Pétain a leader? We'd be better off with your dog. As for being "allowed", as you put it …'

Bernard clasped his bicep and thrust his fist in the

air.

Philippe shook his head sadly. 'France's war is over, Bernard. You'd do well to accept that and make the best of things.'

'You make me feel ashamed, Philippe. Ashamed for you. Truly you do. Will you see your father today?'

'I will. But whether he'll speak to me is another matter.'

Bernard made another breathy chuckle. 'That's because he's a patriot like me. He can't stand the Boche either.'

'I'll tell you what I can't stand,' said Philippe. 'The stink from that septic tank. Goodbye, Bernard.'

He swung his leg over the bicycle and prepared to cycle away, but Bernard caught his arm.

'Hold on, Philippe,' said the garagiste. 'Listen to that.' His expression had become serious. He gazed into the distance, a hand cupped to his ear. 'Didn't you hear it? It's gunfire.'

# 3

Charlie felt the Spitfire shake as the thuds hit, a tight series of blows as rapid and urgent as a drumroll. His heart missed a beat. No mistaking what they were: cannon rounds hammering into his aircraft.

He cursed his stupidity. How could he have let this happen? Where was the attacker? How had neither he nor Kemp seen him – or them – coming?

No time for further thought. Everything now was instinct. He rammed the control column forward. Wherever the German was, he had to lose him, make him think the Spitfire was done for. Which it very well might be, depending on how bad the damage was.

The aircraft stood obediently on its nose and plunged earthward, instantly driving him back in his seat. It was like being kicked in the chest and gut. The straps of the Sutton harness that tethered him to the seat dug into his shoulders. Where an instant before there had been that limpid sky all around, now he was looking straight down at dense scrubland that was rushing towards him at an unholy rate of knots. A glance at the speedo, its needle rocking crazily, confirmed that he was practically off the clock. The racket was deafening – air roaring past and the Merlin engine screaming like a banshee.

He had to level out – not too soon, in case he drew the German back for another go; but soon enough, before that scrubland got much closer. In twenty seconds ... less ... it would be his grave and the Spitfire would be his coffin, for which the narrow cockpit was perfectly sized. Someone stepping on his grave would be the least of his worries.

It was all he could do to combat the momentum of the dive – but the aircraft responded. The scrubland began to slide away beneath him instead of sucking him down. The Spitfire was holding together.

At last there was sky ahead of him again, complete with horizon. Still no sign of the attacker. Perhaps there was only one and Kemp had seen him off or downed him. Or the German had simply withdrawn. It happened like that sometimes – the enemy came from nowhere and disappeared as quickly as he had appeared. A skirmish could be over in seconds; and with it a man's life.

But there was no sign of Kemp either.

Then it happened again. Another rapid succession of dull thuds shook the Spitfire. A neat line of pock marks, each the size of a florin coin, marched across the port wing even as he watched. This time he saw his attacker: the unmistakable silhouette of a 109 swept across the sky. The German rolled to make a return approach and Charlie caught a flash of yellow nose – sure enough, one of the Abbeville squadron. He flipped the Spitfire into a sharp turn and climb on full throttle with boost, guns at fire position and his thumb on the button if only he could get the German in his sights.

Too late. Another series of thuds announced that the German had outfoxed him yet again. Greyish-white trails billowed like swathes of silk from the nose of the Spitfire, accompanied by instant loss of power. The rounds had pierced the glycol coolant tank and penetrated the engine block. The Spitfire was now nothing more than a glider. It was losing height and at any moment could explode into a fireball with him at its core – the fuel tank was just inches in front of his knees.

There was only one course of action he could take, one he had never faced before. It was the decision that broke every airman's heart.

'Sorry, old thing,' he told the Spitfire. 'Time to go our separate ways.'

An icy calm had settled itself upon him, as if he was observing someone else. He released the locking pin of the seat harness, ripped off his flying helmet and reached up to open the cockpit canopy. Another second and he would be falling free through that blue sky – at the mercy of the German if he chose to be unsporting, admittedly, but it was that or be burnt alive. He prepared for the rush of air that would help whip him out.

But the canopy refused to budge. He must have somehow mishandled the emergency release. He tried again, this time half rising from his seat for greater leverage and grabbing the red emergency knob in both hands.

That was when a fierce spasm of pain shot through his left arm, so unexpected and intense that he lost his balance and flopped back down. He heard himself gasp and felt perspiration break out instantly all over his body.

He shook his head to clear the dizziness that the pain had brought and looked down at the arm. All his other actions so far had involved only his right hand and arm; so what was wrong with the left?

A dark stain had appeared on the sleeve of his tunic. The blue-grey cloth had turned black. He stared at it stupidly for a dangerously long moment, unable to decipher what it meant.

The Spitfire continued to descend. It needed his attention. He tore his gaze away, steadied the aircraft and checked again for the 109, then snatched another quick look at the arm. By then he had reached the only conclusion possible. Looking only confirmed it.

The dark stain was blood. He could even smell it now, the unmistakable metallic tang that only blood gave off. He had been shot; the last burst of cannon fire had caught him.

He raised the arm slightly. Even this small movement was agony. The wound was in his upper arm, near the shoulder. A ragged hole in his sleeve showed the entry point. There was something else: a horizontal rip across the front of his tunic. The round had skimmed his chest. Half an inch closer and he would have been torn wide open.

Now, for the first time, he felt panic begin to rise. Fear was always there but always under control; it was panic that could be the real killer, undoing all in an instant. With a deliberate effort he beat it down.

With each second he expected to feel those sickening thuds of cannon fire again. But there was nothing. He scanned the sky in all directions, looking for the 109. Not a thing to be seen, not a wisp of motion anywhere.

It was as if he no longer had any significance to the German, as if he was dead already.

'I'm bloody not,' he said. 'Not by a long bloody way.'

Philippe and Bernard stared at one another. Eiffel cocked his head, ears twitching, even the bent one, and watched his master.

Philippe knew Bernard was right: the rapid thump-thump-thump in the distance could only be heavy gunfire.

'Was it in the village?'

Bernard shook his head. 'It wasn't at ground level. It was up there.' He turned his face to the sky.

'From an aircraft?'

'Boche. A Messerschmitt. Over towards the coast.'

They watched the sky in that direction but they were too close to the forest and the pines were tall. The gunfire was repeated twice more, sounding louder and closer. Behind it Philippe realised that he was hearing two separate engines.

Bernard had reached the same conclusion.

'Dogfight,' he said. 'The other one's a Spitfire.'

'You can tell?'

'I know engines. The Spitfire's in trouble, poor bastard. Hasn't fired back yet, not once.'

They continued to listen, but there was no more gunfire. Now they could hear only one engine. It faded and there was only silence, more ominous than the sounds of battle that had preceded it.

Charlie calculated. He had turned off the ignition and

20

fuel supply but fire remained a danger. There was nothing he could do about that, nor about the possibility that the 109 might return to see its kill through to the end.

How far could he glide without power? He had heard of pilots who had made it all the way back to England from France with dead engines. It was a matter of geometry, wind direction and other factors, certainly including pilot skill, but above all of the altitude at which the glide began. It was time to take his bearings and decide on a destination.

Immediately below lay the broad belt of scrubland he had noted, a couple of miles in width, with the sea to its west. A little further north the scrubland met an area of wooded countryside, a large area, a thick forest. Inland lay a chequerboard in greens and yellows of fields and meadows intersected by roads and dotted with barns and small whitewashed farmhouses and their outbuildings.

The forest was the clue, and north of it a small château ringed by towers: he was in the vicinity of Hardelot, not far from where he had first joined the French coast. The forest was the Forest of Hardelot, which meant he was uncomfortably close to Boulogne with its anti-aircraft guns. He had to take the Spitfire down without going any further north. West was also out: he would have to ditch in the sea to avoid the scrubland; if he survived, which was not guaranteed, he would almost certainly be captured.

But south would bring him back towards Étaples, and the irony of that was more than he could stomach – if he was to come out of this alive, it would never be thanks to Étaples.

'Superstitious, Charlie?' he could hear Kemp saying to that piece of logic. 'Surely not?'

He turned east and inland, making for the fields and farmland. There, perhaps, he stood a chance of avoiding capture and even of making it back to England – there were tales of downed airmen being assisted by French people.

He glimpsed a small hamlet: a church spire, a deserted market square. The gamble now was whether he could find a spot to put down before his failing speed induced a stall.

Each movement he made to control the aircraft sent bolts of pain through his arm. Questions raced through his mind – how seriously was he wounded; how much blood had he lost; how much was he still losing? – but they would have to keep. Directly ahead and now only a couple of hundred feet beneath him lay the fields he needed, one of them a good three or four hundred yards long – his best hope if he could coax the Spitfire that far.

'My God!' exclaimed Bernard. 'There he is!'

Philippe followed his gaze and against the flawless blue sky saw an aircraft falling silently towards the earth – not diving or spinning out of control but descending almost slowly in a graceful glide.

Then it vanished beyond the trees.

Charlie knew it was now or never. No second chance, no repeat approach.

He checked his speed: borderline, just over seventy.

It was too late to lower the undercarriage – his injury had distracted him for precious seconds so that his speed was now too low: the additional drag of the wheels would certainly cause a stall.

He cleared a hedge – only just; another good reason for keeping the wheels tucked away – and at last there was the welcome grass of that long meadow beneath him. Then came an almighty thump as the propeller bit into the earth, quickly followed by a bone-shaking bounce that knocked the top of his head against the canopy as the aircraft bellied onto the ground.

By the time the Spitfire skidded to a stop in a cloud of dusty earth and torn grass, he was unconscious.

# 4

Albert Destry was four years older than his brother Philippe the doctor. He had never been one for book learning; he left that to Philippe and ran the family farm instead. In contrast to Philippe, Albert the farmer was strongly built, as befitted his work. To Philippe's chagrin, Albert still had a full head of glossy black hair. Then again, he was married to Josette, which reassured Philippe that no man's life was perfect. Like Philippe, Albert possessed the proud Destry nose, as indeed did his fifteen-year-old son Fernand, who was the treasure and joy of his life.

Albert farmed because he knew that he belonged to the land, not the other way round. He saw himself not as its master but as its guardian and protector. The land – this earth that he crumbled in his hand each morning and passed through his thick fingers like the beads of a rosary; this corner of France that had welcomed him into the world and in which one day his bones would be laid – was in his care, never in his possession. This was a responsibility that he embraced gladly and was thankful to God for allowing him the privilege of shouldering.

He shouldered other burdens too. They were dark burdens of which he and Josette never spoke, even in the loneliest hours of the night when one of them would wake to find the other weeping softly: two babies, a year apart, whom God had let them see and hold but took from them before the day of their birth was out. But then God relented and gave them Fernand. And if Josette was not the easiest wife for a man, Albert knew the reasons why and his love and forgiveness for her were as rock certain as he hoped God's would be for him.

On that afternoon Albert was forking hay in the west meadow with Fernand, who was as tall as himself now and could work just as hard, when they heard the gunfire. Faint and distant as it was, they recognised it. They saw the two aircraft, but initially only as dots that flickered in the sunlight, one of them plummeting almost vertically towards the earth while the other circled above like a hawk waiting to see where its prey would come down. As father and son watched, the plummeting aircraft took recognisable shape, its fuselage and wings becoming visible. But it remained too high to be identified either in terms of its type or by its markings – RAF roundels or the Luftwaffe's straight-armed black cross, the Balkenkreuz.

'He's had it,' concluded Albert, pausing to lean on his pitchfork. He wiped sweat from his face and shook it from his hair. 'Whoever he is, whatever side.'

But to his surprise the aircraft pulled out of the dive and began to climb back into the sky. Now the other one was rewarded for its patience. It closed in. Albert and Fernand saw tiny flashes of light, like harmless sparks, spring from it, so tiny they could have been the sun glinting on metal or glass. Some moments afterwards the crackle of gunfire reached them: two more bursts. By then billows of smoke were streaming from the climbing aircraft, which had immediately stopped climbing and was falling again, not in a nosedive as before but in a wide spiral.

'So which is he?' wondered Albert again. 'German or English, heh? Why doesn't he bail out?'

'It's a Spitfire,' said Fernand confidently, his eyesight keener than his father's. 'And we should be able to hear his engine by now. But I don't hear anything, Papa. Do you?'

'Then he's lost power. Unless he gets out he really is finished this time. Either way, it's over for him. Maybe he's dead already.'

Evidently the German agreed, for he did not bother to pursue the Spitfire but instead peeled away and was soon gone from view.

'Murdering bastard,' said young Fernand.

Albert frowned at his son. 'Don't let your mother hear that language.'

The Spitfire seemed to hang in the sky but in fact it was descending steadily. The wide circles it was describing began to straighten out.

Again it was Fernand who interpreted the situation.

'He's not finished, Papa,' he declared, excitement rising in his voice. 'He's heading for the east meadow. He's going to try for a landing. Come on, Papa!'

Before Albert could argue, his son had tossed his pitchfork aside and was sprinting back towards the farm and the east meadow. Albert planted his own fork in a rick of hay and set off after him. He was no runner and he knew there was no way he would catch up with the boy.

'Go straight home,' he called after him. 'You hear

me, Fernand? Don't go anywhere near that aircraft –
you go home and wait for me there.'

He glanced up at the sky as he hurried along,
watching the Spitfire as it continued to descend. Then
he looked to see if the German aircraft had returned
but there was no trace of it anywhere. It knew its work
was done.

'Murdering bastard,' muttered Albert.

After leaving Bernard, Philippe Destry and little Eiffel
raced together through the lanes. Like young Fernand,
Philippe was convinced that the aircraft was making
for the farm's east meadow. There had been no
parachute, so the pilot must still be on board. And he
was surely alive – by what kind of fluke could an
unpiloted aircraft bring itself to earth in the way it
seemed to be doing?

But unlike Fernand, Philippe was not at all sure what
the aircraft was. If Bernard was to be believed, it was a
Spitfire, the aircraft that had not returned fire. But
Bernard had probably polished off the best part of a
bottle of Burgundy today, doctor's visit or not, and
there was no telling how accurate his judgements
might or might not be.

It made no difference to Philippe. German or
English, the pilot, if he had indeed survived and
continued to do so, might need medical help. And
German or English, he would receive it from Philippe
Destry if it was within his competence to give it.

So the doctor and his dog raced on as if it was their
lives that were at stake and not that of a man they had
never met and knew nothing of, including whether he

27

was part of the invading force that had taken their country from them.

As Henry Banham departed from the consulting rooms in London's Harley Street, he paused outside on the doorstep to order his thoughts. He turned the fedora about and about in his hands as if it was the embodiment of those thoughts; so preoccupied was he that he forgot for the moment his anxieties about being seen.

Around him the work of clearance continued, but this time he barely heard the racket, barely noticed the unceasing flurry of activity or the rank odour. A workman pushed a wheelbarrow laden with broken masonry past him and apologised when a brick tumbled off, just missing Henry's foot. Henry neither saw nor heard.

This was a bad business. If anything, it was worse than he had anticipated, the diagnosis more severe. All very worrying – more worrying, in fact, than even he had been prepared for. It crossed his mind that he could seek alternative advice – a second opinion, that was the term used. But where was the point in deluding himself? There could be a second opinion, and a third for that matter, but in the end it would be the same opinion. He knew that in his heart. He had seen the symptoms for himself; if he happened upon an opinion that did differ, would he give it any credence? Better simply to get on with things.

Henry sighed. He knew what he had to do. He had to make it an official matter now. Which was something else to worry about.

28

So he dabbed the perspiration from his face, squared his shoulders, noticed the broken brick on the pavement just in time to step over it, discovered the fedora still in his hands and placed it hurriedly on his head, pulled the brim well down and set off to retrieve his car.

# 5

'Wake up!'

The voice, a man's, was muffled, as if reaching Charlie over a great distance or through an obstruction of some kind.

A man's voice? That made no sense. Here was Émilie by his side and they were walking along a narrow street with crooked houses – it felt like Rye, like one of the days they went to Rye – and Émilie, her footsteps ringing on the cobbles, was pushing the pram with their baby son asleep and the hood raised to ward off the sun. She was smiling and talking to Charlie, so it should have been her voice he was hearing, not a man's.

He tried to concentrate on what she was saying but that other voice kept breaking in.

'Snap out of it! You need to get away from here!'

Now Émilie and the pram and the street with its old timbered houses were fading away and there was only darkness. He would sleep now, that was what he wanted more than anything. Very tired. Never been as tired as this. He let himself sink into the darkness.

'Don't do that! Wake up! Come on!'

This time the voice was so forceful that it made him jump. He tried to open his eyes – he realised that they had been shut all along, which was an odd way to go walking – but the brightness made him close them again.

With the brightness the memories began to seep back, like the blood that had seeped into his clothing. Ah, the blood; he remembered the blood. He also remembered cannon rounds pounding his Spitfire. The 109 that came from nowhere. The dry taste of fear. Kemp nowhere to be seen. Terrible anger with himself. Biting back panic, fighting to remain calm. Then the descent in a mortally stricken aircraft. All these things were coming back to him.

He opened his eyes again, fully this time, and forced himself to keep them open. He raised his head. It hurt like hell, even worse when he moved, worse than the worst hangover.

He saw where he was now – if this version of reality could be trusted. He was in the Spitfire. He had landed, a bellyflop. He had been slumped over the instrument panel, which meant he must have been flung forward so that his head bashed into it. How had that happened? Ah yes – he had released his harness. He remembered his head bouncing up against the canopy as well. Little wonder it hurt.

After that he must have lost consciousness but he seemed to be in one piece – though there was the wound in his arm to worry about; that was real enough. He looked down and was shocked to find that the entire sleeve was dark with blood, soaked through. It seemed worse than before. Agony when he moved the arm, his left hand crimson and tacky when he eased off his gauntlet, which also was soaked in blood. A lot of blood had been flowing – might still be flowing, he might still be bleeding. He would have to do something about the arm.

'By all means,' agreed the voice, as if its owner had been listening to his thoughts. 'But first you need to get away from here.'

Charlie jumped again, startled. He tried hard to focus. Things were still pretty foggy in his head. Walking with Émilie in Rye, that was a dream, surely. And this voice that kept cutting in and out like a radio signal – that was just part of the dream; surely it was. But the dream – or hallucination – was over now. So why was the voice still here?

He looked around, not too fast, out of consideration for his head. And here was the damnedest thing, the queerest thing: a man was standing beside the Spitfire, right beside it. He was watching Charlie as calmly as if he was a member of his ground crew and Charlie had just brought the Spitfire safely home to Hawkinge; just standing there looking at him as if nothing in the world could be more natural or ordinary than his presence here. The Spitfire was not a tall aircraft; flat on its belly with the wheels retracted, it was only the height of a man – which was why this particular man was actually gazing down at him through the canopy.

Where on earth had he sprung from?

Another memory stirred: something about the canopy. It had jammed, that was it. Charlie reached up and released the catch. This time it unlocked perfectly normally. The rough landing must have freed it. Using only his right arm and hand, he slid it back. It moved smoothly. At once the heat of the day hit him. After the coolness of the aircraft at twenty thousand feet, it was like a furnace door being flung open.

'Listen to me,' the stranger was saying, his voice clearer with the canopy out of the way. 'Any minute now this place will be swarming with Germans. They'll be looking for you. We need to get you away from here and out of sight.'

Even in his befuddled state, Charlie noted that 'we'.

'Can you get yourself out of this thing?' the stranger continued.

He meant the Spitfire. Charlie nodded in reply, regretting the movement immediately because of the jolt of pain it sent through his head. But the stranger was right: he had no idea how long he had been unconscious, just sitting here in enemy-occupied territory. Even if the 109 was no longer on the prowl, the pilot would certainly have radioed the probable crash location to Abbeville, who must have passed the word to the local Wehrmacht unit by now. They would be on their way; they might even have seen where the Spitfire came down. What better catch than an English airman?

Now his thoughts were becoming clearer. There was one other reason not to hang about, the most pressing of all: he had brought the Spitfire to earth without it turning into a fireball but it could still explode at any moment. Time was not on his side.

He dropped the side door open, made sure he was free of the parachute harness, wrapped his good arm about the top of the front windscreen and the mirror mount, and hauled himself to his feet. Despite his care, pain shot through his left arm anyway. But on his feet he was able to slip his life jacket off with minimal further hurt to the arm; getting out of the cramped

33

cockpit was easier without the bulky jacket. He stepped out to the inboard walkway of the wing and from there to the ground – normally a hop down, but not this time with the aircraft pancaked.

The stranger was already forty or fifty yards away.

'This way,' he called.

Maybe, thought Charlie; or maybe not.

He took a hurried look around, clear-headed enough now to prefer to make his own decision. Behind the Spitfire a deep gouge like a ploughed strip marked the path it had taken on this its final landing. Beyond the meadow there was open farmland in three directions, and in the distance a farmhouse. France was a large country and the distances between rural neighbours could be great. This particular farmhouse was about half a mile away, the only habitation visible in the entire landscape. Not far from it he could see the shiny tin roof of at least one barn, shimmering in the haze of heat. Even now someone might be watching from that farmhouse or the barn or any of the fields surrounding the meadow.

There was no safety in any of those directions, nowhere he might hide, nowhere he could reach unseen in broad daylight, not even the barn, however tempting it was.

To the north-west, however, and also about half a mile distant, stretched a broad expanse of woodland, its dark outline wavering in the heat. It was the forest he had seen from the air, the Forest of Hardelot. No farmer or farmer's wife or labourer there to tell tales, no German officer billeted there, just a place where a man might be able to lie low for a time.

And it was exactly where the stranger was already heading.

Charlie knew he had no choice; there was nowhere else to go. So ignoring the blinding pain in his arm and in his head that every step of that seemingly endless half mile cost him, he ran after this complete stranger who had materialised from nowhere.

He reached the cover of the forest just in time. An almighty whoomph sounded behind him and a pulse of scorching air surged across the meadow and rippled past him through the trees.

He crouched down among thick growths of gold-tinted brush and glistening ground ivy. The aircraft lifted from the earth for a brief moment, seeming to be seeking its natural element one last time, then collapsed back down and split in half, a broken bird.

In an adjacent field, as if lamenting its passing, scores of crows rose in a great flock, their mournful caws and the beating of their wings drowned by the noise of the blast.

Bursts of yellow and red and orange flame raced along the Spitfire's fuselage and wings, and a great plume of oily black smoke curled into the sky. Then a series of sharp reports like firecrackers signalled that the ammo in the ammunition boxes was beginning to explode – not a single round of which, to Charlie's shame, he had managed to fire today.

Some hero he was; some ace.

He bade the aircraft farewell, for certain this time, and turned towards the deep shadows of the forest and the safety he hoped they would provide.

# 6

Albert practically fell through the farmhouse doorway. To his relief Fernand was there with Josette. Albert's father, known to one and all simply as Pépé, was also there, in his armchair. As ever. He had a regal way of occupying the armchair, threadbare though it was, as if it was his throne and all those around him were his subjects. Reluctantly he turned his head – adorned with the usual Destry nose – towards his son as he arrived and studied him in silence for a moment, then lost interest, as he usually did in both his sons, and looked away.

'What's going on, Albert?' demanded Josette. She pushed a strand of dark curly hair from her face. It tumbled right back. The handsome looks that had first drawn Albert to her were still there if a person took the trouble to look for them beneath the patina of time and hardship and loss.

'First Fernand, now you,' she said. 'Are you both mad? Look at yourself, you're sweating like a boar in heat.'

'Didn't you hear the gunfire?'

Josette shrugged non-committally and resumed turning the handle of the butter churn. Butter had to be made; gunfire did not have to be heard. The sinews in her arm and broad shoulder tightened and loosened as she leant into the task.

Work was Josette's religion. It defined, justified and set the rhythm of her existence. It was what she had been put on this earth to do. She had been born on a farm, she was raised on that farm and bent her back to her fair share of everything that had to be done on that farm – son or daughter made no difference – she married a farmer as she had always known she would, and changed not her life or her principles but merely her allegiance to which farm and whose hectares benefited from her labour. If she had ever missed a day's work in her life – and no one could remember such a day, childbearing aside – it had not been a happy or fulfilling day for her. As for the childbearing, after holding her two dead children in her arms, on each occasion she had returned to work the next day, taking only an hour or two away from the fields and the cattle for the funeral arrangements. This was not hard-heartedness; it was just that she was as rooted in the needs of the day as were the animals that she tended in her pastures. The work was always there; so she had always to be there too.

She browbeat and censured Albert as naturally and instinctively as breathing but she loved him as much as he loved her. They had been through too much together for either to be complete without the other. The vine branched but there was only the one root. She knew this was something that no one but she and Albert understood behind their bickering. She also knew the suspicion with which her brother-in-law Philippe regarded her; but this was the price of daring to stand between two Destry brothers and she paid it willingly.

'The Germans are always shooting at something,' she told her husband now as he stood waiting for an answer, as restless as a child. 'If it's not us, it's rabbits or deer. It's all the same to them – target practice, as if they're boys in a fairground. Anyway, I've just come up from the sous-sol. You hear nothing down there.' She reflected for a moment. 'But something made the house shake, I can tell you that – I thought we had an earthquake. Then Fernand came charging in with some stupid story and practically knocked me down –'

'It's not a story, Maman!'

'Did the aircraft land in the meadow?' asked Albert impatiently.

Josette had decided not to like his tone. 'What aircraft? I told you – how would I know what's going on out there? I've got my work to do.'

'She hasn't bothered to look, and she stopped me looking too,' grumbled Fernand. 'Wouldn't even let me get to a window.'

Pépé sucked at what were left of his teeth, a signal that he was about to dispense information or opinion, or, if his audience was especially lucky, both, and shifted in his threadbare throne.

'I've seen it,' he volunteered. 'I'd just come out of the privy and there it was, on its way down. Crash landing. Wheels up, they call it. It's in the meadow but you won't see it from a window. You need to go to the end of the yard. It's English – not that anyone in this family cares. See, Albert, the English are willing to stand up to the Boche, which is more than can be said for your brother or you.'

Albert opened his mouth to reply but a huge

38

swooshing boom rattled the windows. He and the others ducked instinctively. Josette dropped the butter churn.

'Another earthquake?' she shrieked. 'God save us!' She looked in despair at the pool of buttermilk spreading across the stone floor and dashed to fetch her mop.

'Stay here, all of you,' instructed Albert.

He hurried outside. The first thing he saw was a thick plume of black smoke spiralling into the sky. He went to the end of the yard as Pépé had advised and there an extraordinary sight met his eyes. In the middle of the meadow, perhaps a kilometre downhill from him, an inferno was blazing. At its heart was a fighter aircraft with RAF markings, or at any rate the charred outlines of those markings. It lay completely flat on the ground, just as old Pépé had said, like a stallion whose legs had folded under it. Flames danced over the fuselage and wings.

As he watched the blaze he recalled a day when he and Fernand had gone to Boulogne to buy animal feed. Every supplier's response was the same: the Germans had commandeered everything. Fernand was close to tears. Then, as yet another merchant shook his head, there came a fearsome roar overhead. Like everyone else in the wholesaler's, father and son flattened themselves on the floor. Two machines like the one he was looking at now swooped past at unbelievable speed and at rooftop height. Even though this was before the German defences at the port had been strengthened, it was an audacious incursion.

Fernand, delirious with joy, had chanted 'Spitfires!

Spitfires!' until his father hushed him. But on the train home the boy was still full of the incident.

'England will fix the Boche, Papa. You just wait.'

'Keep your voice down,' said Albert, fearful of who might be listening, of who might know who they were and report them. 'Be quiet,' he told his son, and felt ashamed to be setting such an example of cowardice. But what choice did he have? If his first child, also a son, had lived, he would have been old enough last year to be conscripted; and could be dead by now in consequence. God protect Fernand.

A sudden series of sharp cracks sounded from the direction of the burning wreck and brought Albert back to the present. With a flash of anxiety he realised that the aircraft's ammunition was exploding. He stepped back quickly into the lee of the farmhouse. A noise behind him made him turn. He was just in time to grab Fernand as the boy tried to run past to look down the meadow.

'It's dangerous here, Fernand. Go back indoors.'

'But Papa, all that smoke – is the aircraft on fire? What if the pilot's trapped inside?'

'If that's the case, there's nothing we can do for him. I'm sorry. Bullets are flying in all directions. Go back to the house.'

But Fernand slipped like a fish from his grasp. He glared at his father, anger in his eyes. The transition was so sudden and unexpected that Albert stood stock-still, staring back at him in alarm.

'Papa, that man was fighting for us. Are you going to let him die?'

'The aircraft's ablaze. It's an inferno. We'd never get

anywhere near it.'

'So you'll do nothing. You of all people.'

'Me of all people? What do you mean by that?'

'I know what's going on, Papa. You and Uncle Philippe. I'm not soft in the head like old Pépé.'

Albert's heart skipped a beat. 'Heh? What about me and Philippe?'

Fernand drew a deep breath. 'I know about the men.'

It was enough. More than enough. Albert caught his son by both arms. He looked quickly around. There was no one else in the yard, no one within earshot.

'You don't know anything, Fernand. Do you understand? There were no men. Forget it all, whatever you think you know.'

'How can I, Papa? I don't want to. No men? I saw them. Large as life. Why would I choose to forget? Why would I behave as if I'm ashamed of you? Is that what you want – that I should be ashamed of my father?'

They stood there, father and son locked together, their hearts beating so hard that each thought the other must hear, until gradually the grip in which Albert held his son became an embrace.

'Oh Fernand,' he said, gently. A boy could become a man without his father even noticing.

'It's all right, Papa,' said Fernand. 'I won't tell. Not Maman, not Pépé. Not anyone.'

'I know you won't. You're a good son. It's not telling that worries me, Fernand. Knowing is bad enough.'

Eiffel got to the farmyard before Philippe. What the

41

little dog lacked in length of leg he made up for with enthusiasm and his well-used shortcuts through the undergrowth. He bounded up to Albert and Fernand and was bouncing happily about them when Philippe arrived.

'Is that the aircraft?' said Philippe as he dismounted, breathless from his exertions, his gaze fixed on the column of smoke. 'Whose is it? Did the pilot –'

He broke off. He saw the expression on his brother's face as the farmer turned to look at him, his arms still about his son. There was anguish; but pride too. Albert flicked his gaze towards Fernand, then looked back at Philippe, his mouth set. To the doctor the message was as clear as day. No words were needed between brother and brother. Philippe nodded to signify his understanding.

'It's an English aircraft,' said Albert. 'Don't know if the pilot got out. Seems unlikely.'

Philippe put his arms round his brother and nephew.

'If he did get out and if we can help him, we will,' he said. He clasped Fernand's shoulder. 'The three of us.'

# 7

After the brilliant sunshine in the meadow and the glare of the flames consuming the Spitfire, it took Charlie some moments to adjust to the dimness of the forest. He rose to his feet and looked around. Most of the trees that surrounded him were pines but here on the outer margins he saw a scattering of broadleaved varieties that were fighting to survive – birch and ash, a few oaks. The ground was a spongy bed of pine needles overlaid with ferns and brush. He saw stands of hazel, the clusters of slender sawn trunks that crowded their bases evidence that they were being coppiced by local woodmen. Here and there sat stacks of firewood, neatly arranged and awaiting collection.

The place was still and serene, like a workplace in which today was not a working day. The air here was cool after the smothering heat of the meadow and when he drew a deep breath he felt his lungs swell in his chest. He was alive; despite everything, he was still alive. A wave of exhaustion suddenly washed over him. He fought it. For a moment Émilie was by his side again. Perhaps it was her perfume he could smell and not the sweet, woody fragrance of the forest. Perhaps it was his son's laughter he heard and not the soft cooing of wood pigeons.

But thinking of them only made matters worse, provoking an ache within him that hurt more than the throbbing headache or the pain in his arm. It was the bitter ache of loss, an emptiness that stretched his soul to breaking point.

He peered through the shadows, wondering where the man had gone.

'Over here,' said the now-familiar voice, so quietly it might have been in his mind. It was right on cue, as if its owner had waited for him to be ready, not wanting to intrude on his private moment of yearning. The man was standing beneath a tall pine further into the woodland, just beyond where a shaft of light filtered through the trees. In his dark clothing he was almost invisible against the browns and dark green shadows of the place.

It was the first chance Charlie had to take a proper look at him. There was little to remark. He saw a man who was about his own height and probably much the same age. A very ordinary man as far as he could see, with nothing to distinguish him from a dozen other men in any crowd. Regular features of the kind that people tended to consider good-looking. But pass him by and forget all about him, sit beside him in the barber's queue and not recognise him later: that kind of man. Brown hair, a few days' stubble on his cheeks and chin, hard to be sure about the eye colour at this distance, but dark, probably brown. A stillness about him. Wearing a dark shirt, brownish, and dark trousers, also brownish. A brownish sort of man altogether; a forgettable sort of man.

He gazed levelly back at Charlie, perfectly aware he was being studied but his expression calm and impassive.

44

'Come on, follow me,' he said, and made to turn away, to go deeper into the forest.

Charlie held his ground. 'I need to see to my arm before I bleed to death.'

'No time for that. The Germans will be here soon. In any case, the bleeding's stopped. It's been stopped for a while.'

'How do you know?'

'I checked.'

Charlie felt a shiver of unease. He forced a laugh. 'How? Looked me over while I was out for the count?'

The man had moved from the shadow of the pine tree.

'That's right,' he said. 'I thought it wise.'

'Well, thanks for that. Thanks also for your help back there. I wasn't quite compos mentis.'

'Only to be expected. You took a couple of nasty knocks to the head – I had a look at those too.'

'Good of you. The name's Charlie Quinn, by the way. That's about all I'm allowed to tell you, I'm afraid.' He smiled apologetically. 'That's war for you.'

As he was speaking, he had planted his right foot on a fallen tree trunk and was reaching down to his boot, tugging at its high sides as if to loosen it.

'I know your name already,' came the reply. The man had come closer. 'It was written on your life jacket. You're wearing a wedding ring, so you're married. You have a photo in your pocket, presumably of your family. Right now you're trying to get hold of that pistol in your boot. You're also carrying a spare magazine for it, a knife and some French francs. You had a map in the aircraft but you left it behind. A

45

compass too, also gone up in smoke. No matter – you don't need either, now that I'm here.'

Charlie withdrew the Browning semi-automatic from his boot. Its weight suggested that it was still fully loaded, that the stranger had not emptied the magazine. Now he aimed the gun at the man, who had again managed to draw closer without Charlie hearing or seeing him do so.

'Stay where you are. No closer,' Charlie told him. 'I'm glad of your help, don't get me wrong, but searching me – that wasn't a nice thing to do.'

'On the contrary, perfectly proper in the circumstances. Essential procedure to make sure you're not carrying anything of potential use to the enemy. And I have enough military experience to know a man should be armed if he ends up in enemy territory. I was just making sure you are. Everything I've done was in your own interests.'

'Then you won't mind telling me who you are and what you're doing here.'

The stranger spread his arms. 'Of course not, but look, you can see I don't have a weapon. Your suspicions are understandable but I promise you they're unnecessary. I've done nothing but help you. I pose no threat. The very opposite, as it happens.'

'I'll decide that for myself. Who are you?'

'You've told me your name and now you want to know mine. Is that it?'

'Never mind your name. You could invent any name you like and I'd be none the wiser. Who you actually are, that's a bigger question. What's an Englishman doing here?'

'I could ask you the same thing.'

'I didn't choose to be here.'

'Perhaps I didn't either. Yet here we both are.'

'What's your military experience? Are you an airman?'

The man glanced towards the burning wreck. 'I've never even been in one of those. Never left the ground, you might say.'

'So you're an infantryman. You surely haven't been in France since Dunkirk?'

Many men had been left behind during the chaos and confusion of that evacuation; Charlie knew that. Some had been taken as prisoners of war but others had avoided capture; of these, some were still managing to find their way back to England, in ones and twos. Theirs were among the stories that gave him hope for his own return.

'It's true I've been in France a while,' the man said.

'Oh yes? How long?'

The stranger said nothing.

'Why did you endanger yourself by approaching my aircraft? It could have blown us both up.'

'Fortunately for you, it didn't.'

'Fortunately for you too.'

The stranger shrugged indifferently. 'You got out in time, that's all that matters. But you'd be ashes by now if I hadn't made you come round, pull yourself together. So you see, you can trust me, Charlie.'

'You might have a different fate in mind for me.'

'Like what? You think I might be leading you into a trap? I might be a German agent or sympathiser?'

'The thought occurred. Maybe you're not English at

all. Maybe your military experience has nothing to do with Dunkirk.'

'You're not thinking straight. If I'm working for the Germans, I could have blown your head off with your own gun or held you at gunpoint until they get here – which they will very soon, incidentally.' He sighed. 'I only want to help you. You need somewhere safe until things calm down. Your arm is all right for now but it does need proper medical attention. And you want to get back home, don't you? You've got that on your mind, unless I'm much mistaken. Well, you need help with all of that. You can't go it alone, believe me.'

'Get back home': the words hit Charlie hard.

'And this is where you come in?'

'If you let me.'

'You haven't answered any of my questions.'

'Well, just like you can tell me your name but nothing else, maybe there are things I can't tell you. That's war for both of us, Charlie.'

'Very clever.'

The stranger shrugged, another take-it-or-leave-it shrug. Again he said nothing. He had a knack of doing that.

'Odd that you just happened to be here when I came down. How do you explain that?'

'Sometimes things just work out. Maybe someone's looking out for you.'

Charlie became aware of the distant sound of engines. German vehicles – just as the stranger had been warning.

The man's gaze shifted to the landscape beyond the trees. 'You need to make your mind up now, Charlie.

The Germans will expect to find your incinerated remains in your aircraft. When they don't, they'll start looking for you. So either you put the gun away and follow me or you're on your own. If you plan to shoot me, now's the time – but it'll have to be in the back. That's something else you can decide for yourself.'

He strode off.

Suddenly Charlie felt very alone. The tiredness was back again. Loss of blood, he told himself, together with the physical effect of his injuries. Then there was the shock of what he had been through, plus the decline that came after huge quantities of adrenalin had been pumping through the human body. It was an effect every pilot knew well.

He watched as the man vanished among the trees. Who was this character? What was he doing here, in the middle of a French field, in the middle of nowhere, in the middle of a war, just when a Spitfire came crashing to earth?

But whoever he was, there was something in what he said – he could have put a bullet in Charlie's head or turned him in. He had done neither. Perhaps he was Charlie's best chance.

And besides, human company was human company.

So Charlie made the Browning safe, slipped it into his waistband and hastened after the stranger.

Albert ventured again to the end of the yard, having cautioned Fernand to remain with Philippe. To his relief the boy did not argue.

It was now several minutes since the ammunition had stopped exploding. Hopefully there would be no more. Even so, Albert was not inclined to take chances. He peered cautiously round the corner of the farmhouse before stepping clear to survey the scene in the meadow properly.

Nothing seemed to have changed. The aircraft was still burning. Smoke still poured into the sky. And just as before, there was no evidence of any human activity.

'What can you see, Papa?'

'Just the aircraft on fire. I don't see the pilot.'

'Can I look now?'

Albert nodded. His son and Philippe joined him. Eiffel, who had stayed with his master, trotted along at Philippe's heels and sat down on the concrete for a scratch. Albert put his arm about Fernand's shoulder.

'The pilot must be dead,' he said. 'No one could survive that blaze. I'm sorry, Fernand. There was no way we could have saved him.'

'So what do we do now?'

But at that moment Eiffel stopped scratching and jumped to his feet. He turned in the general direction of the village and barked loudly several times, his left ear erect and his tail quivering. Gradually the barks subsided into a disgruntled growl.

Recognising the warning, the men and the boy fell silent and listened. At first the only sounds apart from Eiffel growling were the steady crackling of the flames as the Spitfire continued to burn, and clattering and complaints from the farmhouse kitchen where Josette was mopping up the mess from the overturned butter churn. But after a moment they heard the first low drone of truck engines, far distant to begin with but slowly growing louder and closer. Eiffel continued to growl, pacing back and forth with his legs straight and stiff, which gave him something of a military air.

'What do we do?' Fernand said again.

'Nothing,' said Philippe. He looked at his brother. 'There's nothing for us to do.'

Albert shrugged his agreement.

Philippe removed his cycle clips and crouched down to scratch the wiry fur behind Eiffel's ears.

'Our German friends are on their way, Fernand. This is their show now. We leave it to them.'

It was no easy task for Charlie to keep the man in sight as he followed at a pace dictated by his need to avoid stumbling or banging his arm against branches. But as they went deeper into the forest he saw that it was worth the effort. Soon the meandering course that the stranger navigated ceased to follow any path – because there were no longer any paths to follow. Nor were there any more of those tidy stacks of firewood, and the growths of hazel had been left alone, as if the woodmen did not bother with them.

'No one comes this far in,' the stranger was saying over his shoulder as he waited for Charlie to catch up. He seemed to know what was going through Charlie's mind, answering questions he had scarcely formulated, let alone spoken aloud – though never the ones that Charlie had asked earlier. 'No reason for them to do so. People can get what they need on the fringes of the forest – firewood, mushrooms, berries, the occasional deer.'

Gradually the sound of engines faded to nothing,

reduced by distance and absorbed by the trees. The only sounds Charlie could hear were the buzzing of insects and his own clumsy crashing through the undergrowth, a contrast with the stranger's effortless and silent progress.

The stranger came to a halt.

'Here we are,' he said. He was looking down at the ground just ahead of where he was standing in a small clearing. Silvery rays of sunlight played through the trees around him.

Charlie was still about thirty yards away. He could see nothing of any note, just the woodland floor with its thick bed of pine needles, cones, fallen branches and twigs. The only feature marking it as different from any other part of the forest through which they had travelled was the carpet of dead leaves from oaks and birches that had succeeded in establishing themselves here.

Then he came closer and looked again.

# 8

The Destry farmyard was the only place from which the meadow could be reached by vehicle, the other fields along the lane being bordered by high hedges, runs of wire fencing and steep earth banks overgrown with dog roses and tangled briars.

The Germans rolled up to the farmyard in three open-backed trucks. Exhaust fumes and clouds of choking dust swirled around them as if they belonged to some infernal region of the underworld; which, Philippe reflected, was not too far from the truth. He counted thirty troopers as they piled out of the vehicles in a melee of squealing brakes, clattering steel-heeled boots, rifles and steel helmets, this racket accompanied by a litany of shouted commands from their officer.

Philippe sighed as the yard filled. There was no apology, no request to enter. There never was with these invaders, wherever they chose to plant their hobnail boots.

The troopers paid no heed to the two men, the boy and the little growling dog but clomped past them across the farmyard as though it was their own parade ground, then spread out in a line as they entered the meadow, advancing in formation towards the burning Spitfire. Unlike Philippe and Albert and Fernand, they were equipped for the task, some of them carrying fire extinguishers. The officer barked more of his orders and they began to spray the aircraft from end to end while the others stood guard, rifles aimed at the Spitfire.

'Do they think someone's going to leap out and attack them?' said Philippe.

'If there's any fuel left in the tank, their guns won't save them when it goes up,' said his brother.

'No harm in hoping,' said Fernand.

But the fuel had already gone; there were no explosions.

Each time the fire seemed to be out, fresh flames would spring to life, hidden at first by the bright sunshine until they blossomed into tongues of red and steely blue, and the troopers had to dash forward and tackle them all over again. The sun continued to beat down. In due course more extinguishers had to be fetched from the trucks.

When the flames were finally out, the perspiring troopers traipsed back and forth between the farmyard and the aircraft for another while, lugging buckets of water from the pump with which to cool the hot wreck.

'Why are they bothering?' said Albert. 'Why go to so much trouble for a heap of burnt-out wreckage?'

'They'll send it by train to Germany,' said Fernand knowledgeably. 'Their aircraft designers will want to see if they can learn anything they can put to use in their own aircraft. They extinguished the fire instead of letting it burn out in case there are any documents they could salvage – attack plans, technical material.'

Albert raised an eyebrow, impressed. Philippe smiled.

The column of smoke that had stained the sky was

gone at long last; only clouds of steam rose from the remains of the aircraft.

Eventually a couple of the troopers got close enough to the blackened shell to be able to peer into the cockpit. After a moment they returned to the officer and conferred with him. The officer himself went up to the cockpit. Even at a distance the atmosphere of tension was apparent.

'What's all that about, heh?' muttered Albert. 'What have they found?'

'I think I know,' said Fernand.

'Then tell us,' said Philippe. An idea had taken shape in his own mind but he wanted to hear what his nephew thought. Fernand was a bright lad.

'Perhaps it's not what they've found,' said Fernand. 'Perhaps it's what they haven't found. I don't think the pilot's there – his remains, I mean. I think they've just discovered that and they're not happy about it. If I'm right, it means he got away from the aircraft before it exploded.'

'You think he escaped?' said Albert. 'That's not possible. How could he? We'd have seen him. We've been here, watching all the time.'

'Actually, no, we haven't,' said Philippe, shaking his head slowly. 'Not every minute. Think about it.'

They thought.

'My God,' said Albert. 'You're right.'

'He did it, he got away,' said Fernand jubilantly.

'My God,' said Albert again as the implications of this conclusion began to sink in. He looked at his brother.

'I know, I know,' said Philippe, agreeing with

Albert's unspoken comment. 'But let's wait and see. And don't look too interested. You especially, Fernand. Our friends in the meadow wouldn't like that.'

He bent down and scratched behind Eiffel's ears.

It was as if Charlie had crossed into another world.

He stepped over the little stream to which the stranger had brought him. It was less than a yard wide and was visible above ground for only about a dozen yards, emerging from a dip in the forest floor and disappearing in the same way. It trickled gently but steadily and, with few rocks to interrupt its course, was barely audible over the birdsong and the whir of insects that hovered above it.

Charlie knelt down and looked into the bubbling water. It was clean and perfectly clear. It was also blissfully cool, as he found when he dipped his hand into it and sipped; no drink had ever been so sweet and pure. He realised how parched he was. He drank his fill, then doused his face, head and neck to wash the blood from his forehead and the back of his head.

Like all fighter pilots, he wore a silk scarf. This was not flashiness; the softness of the silk protected his neck from being chafed by his collar as he craned around endlessly to check his surroundings and watch for enemy aircraft – something he had signally failed to do well enough today.

He had a different use for the scarf now. He got himself out of his tunic and ripped his shirtsleeve to expose the wound in his arm, then used the scarf to wash away the dried blood, taking care not to start the bleeding again.

The wound was about half an inch in diameter, more or less circular. Its jagged edges suggested it had been made by shrapnel – a lucky escape since a Messerschmitt cannon round, unless it had only grazed him, could have taken his arm off.

The stranger watched his efforts in silence from the edge of the clearing until the moment when Charlie unsheathed his knife. This implement was intended not as a weapon but as a survival tool. Instead of a point it had a rounded end. It was for cutting parachute cords, and the rounded end made it safe for bomber crews in their inflatable dinghy if they ditched.

He began to probe the perimeter of the wound with a fingertip, holding the knife at the ready, but the stranger had done his trick of coming closer without him noticing.

'Don't do that,' he told Charlie.

'Why not?'

'You're thinking about cutting the wound open. Don't. Cleaning it up is one thing, butchery is another.'

'There's shrapnel in there, I have to get it out.'

'With that? You'll rip your arm apart. And knock yourself unconscious all over again. Then you really will bleed to death. There's a better way.'

'So tell me.'

'You'll scc.'

'Will that be before or after I develop septicaemia?'

'The arm will be all right. Have I misled you in any way so far? There's something you need to see to, something more important. You're at a low ebb, your judgement isn't at its best. You need to rest and rebuild your strength – for that you need to make yourself safe. That's your priority, Charlie. I said I'd bring you to a safe place and here it is. I haven't done that merely for you to slice yourself open and die here.'

Charlie put the knife away. The man was right about the folly of using it. Another knack he seemed to have: that of being right. For he was also right about something else: the Germans would search the forest. Again Charlie was running out of time – he needed somewhere to hide.

He tied the scarf about his arm as a bandage and looked again at this place he had been brought to. A safe place, the stranger claimed. On the far side of the clearing the ground fell away sharply, a drop of four or five feet caused by an earth slippage long ago. A great oak tree, its trunk almost two yards wide, stood right where the cleft had occurred. Half of its roots arched over the edge, stretching down to anchor themselves in the shelf of earth below, where they had thickened and fused together. The result was a natural shelter, a roof that was now densely covered in dry leaves, twigs and moss. And was large enough for a man. A safe place.

Charlie turned around to look for the stranger. Who now was nowhere to be seen.

He slid down the slope and pushed himself beneath the roots feet first and on his stomach. It was the first time the stranger had disappeared. But Charlie was fine with that. Sooner or later the man would be back. Charlie knew that as surely as he knew his own name. He did not know how he knew it; he just did, and that was enough, a certitude within him with which he was too tired to argue.

Exhaustion overwhelmed him. Within a minute he was asleep.

# 9

Matters in the east meadow were taking a different turn. And not a turn for the good.

The officer came marching back up to the farmyard, flanked by a dozen or so of the troopers. This time it was Philippe and Albert and Fernand at whom some of the rifles were levelled. To emphasise the point, the officer drew his pistol, a Luger.

'Against the wall,' he commanded, in heavily accented French.

'You can't order us about,' protested Albert.

The German disagreed. He slammed the muzzle of the Luger hard against Albert's forehead. Fernand cried out in alarm. Philippe caught the boy and held him firmly. Albert's eyes were wide with fear.

'Schnell!' shouted the officer.

Philippe grabbed his brother's arm and, still holding Fernand, backed the three of them towards the wall.

Eiffel had begun to bark at a piercingly high pitch, lips drawn back and teeth bared. He crouched, ready to spring to the attack. The officer saw what was coming and turned the gun on the small dog.

'No!' screamed Philippe. He released his hold on Albert and Fernand, and lunged at the German. The officer swung the Luger and would have shattered his cheekbone had Philippe not raised his arm in time to ward off the blow. He fell back, clutching his arm.

Eiffel yelped loudly and fled, tail between his legs, moving faster than his master or anyone else had ever seen before.

The troopers roared with laughter but the officer rounded on them and snapped out an order. The grins immediately left their faces. The troopers made their way towards the barns and outbuildings. Some headed to the farmhouse.

The officer brandished the Luger until Philippe and the others were right against the wall. At his nod, two troopers came forward and took over from him, holding the captives at gunpoint.

'Are they going to shoot us?' whispered Fernand.

'Schweigen Sie!' rasped one of the troopers. Shut up.

'No, they won't shoot us,' said Philippe. Sweat ran down from his glistening head and into his eyes. He brushed it away and scowled at the trooper. 'Not even this moron will do that. But they're going to search the farm.'

'Including the barns?'

Philippe looked at his nephew. A bright lad indeed.

'They're bound to,' he told him. 'But don't worry – they won't find anything.'

'Schweigen Sie!'

This time the trooper thrust his rifle against Philippe's chest. Philippe decided he had pushed his luck far enough. It would be nice to finish the day in the same overall state as he had begun it: alive.

The troopers had entered the farmhouse. There were shouts of 'Raus! Raus!' and Josette and Pépé came tumbling out. Pépé's regal bearing was gone. He seemed either unable or disinclined to find any words other than swear words. Josette was limping. She had lost one of her wooden-soled shoes and had stepped on broken crockery or glass. The foot was dripping blood.

'This is your fault,' she hissed at her husband.

Albert was still quaking from his encounter with the Luger. His fingers explored the circular bruise it had left.

'Me, Josette? Why me?' he pleaded. 'What have I done?'

'Schweigen!' called the trooper.

'I don't know, Albert, not yet, but it's bound to be your fault.' She turned to Philippe. 'Look at this – my foot's practically severed. Tell them you're a doctor and I need urgent treatment. God alone knows what they're doing to our house. I've got work to do. Philippe – my foot, pay attention!'

'Schweigen!'

The muzzle of the rifle lodged beneath Josette's chin. She whimpered and then became silent.

Philippe heard Albert sigh; whether from sympathy for her plight or relief at her silence was unclear to him. But not for the first time he blessed his own bachelorhood.

Eiffel tore across the meadow like a small white comet, giving a wide berth to the smoking ruin of the aircraft and to the troopers, who reminded him too much of the frightening men he was fleeing from. The amused soldiers watched him as he flew past, some whistling and others cheering him on, but nothing was going to persuade him to detour towards them or slow his dash to safety. His nostrils twitched with many strange odours, none of them the odours of nature or resembling anything he had ever encountered before. Nor were they odours he wanted to investigate. On the contrary, they drove him all the faster, to get away from them.

He felt safer when he reached the trees. His spirits lifted. The forest was a place he understood, with its quietness and its good smells and its dappled light. When he came upon the stream he lapped its cool water gratefully to slake his thirst. Then he sat back on his haunches and had a thorough scratch to try and rid his coat of some of the debris it had accumulated during his dash. He sniffed the sweet air and took in its many scents, all of them now the usual comforting blends, all of them familiar – apart from one, which was new to him. But since it was also unthreatening, he wandered about for a while, poking and pawing here and there to his heart's content, and had a pee against the large oak tree at the edge of the clearing, where the land fell sharply away.

He scrambled down to the base of the canopy formed by the oak's overhanging roots, crept through the opening he discovered and licked the face of the man who was fast asleep there.

# 10

While the Destry farm was being searched and the family held at gunpoint, a trooper had taken one of the trucks back to the barracks. Now he returned, bringing two large Alsatian dogs and their handlers. The dogs were muscular, yellow-toothed beasts, panting and slavering; their handlers could barely keep hold of the long chains that served as leashes.

'Not good,' whispered Philippe to his brother as the monsters passed, saliva streaming from their mouths, tongues lolling from their powerful jaws. 'Not good at all.'

The guards had become bored and were now distracted by the arrival of the dogs; besides, they were tired and hot from their firefighting work, and their sickly complexions suggested to Philippe that they were probably feeling more than a little woozy from the stomach-turning stink of oily smoke. No telling how much they might have inhaled. So either they failed to hear his whisper or it was too much effort to do anything about it. He took advantage of this small freedom.

'The dogs will hunt him down, Albert.'

'For certain,' whispered his brother. 'And if they don't tear him apart, these thugs will.'

'After all he's been through,' added young Fernand. 'All for nothing. Merde.'

'Language, Fernand.'

At last the search of the farm was over. The officer emerged from the house. His men had found nothing. The troopers who had searched the barns and outbuildings returned. They shook their heads in reply to his gruff questions. The disappointed officer said something to the soldiers guarding the family. The men lowered their rifles and went off to join their comrades in the meadow, who were now watching as the Alsatians snuffled their way around the blackened and sooty remains of the English aircraft.

'Is that it?' asked Albert, addressing the departing officer's back. He rubbed at the bruise on his forehead. 'We get our home back now? An apology would be nice.'

Pépé loosed off a fresh stream of obscenities.

'Hush, Pépé,' said Philippe automatically. He wondered if Eiffel was safe.

Josette had bound her foot in a cleaning rag that she carried in her apron. She turned to Philippe.

'This foot –'

'Come on, Maman,' urged Fernand. 'Let's see what the Boche have done to our home.'

The sorry little band trailed back to the farmhouse.


Down in the meadow the Alsatians were having a difficult time.

The air remained heavy with the stench of the burnt-out aircraft – paint and metal consumed in the flames along with the undercarriage tyres, the myriad hoses and sheathed cables that constituted the machine's arteries and ligaments, the Bakelite and plastics of its instruments and radio equipment, the parachute silk and the fabrics of the harness that had once held Charlie Quinn secure, and a hundred other materials and substances that had all gone up in smoke. There was the pungent sting of petrol and engine oils that had been combusted but still left their cloying presence in the atmosphere. Cordite fumes continued to leak from the ammunition boxes in the wings and were creeping directly into the grass.

To complicate matters further, the ground was sodden with the chemicals released by the fire extinguishers; these compounds had now been trodden through by thirty-odd pairs of boots that had spread their essence far and wide. The run-off from the water poured by the troopers had washed the chemicals and the cordite and the odours of all the incinerated substances throughout the immediate scene and down the slope of the meadow towards the forest.

So the dogs circled around and around, their confused snouts to the wet ground. The creatures had no reference point, no item of clothing that bore the scent of the man they were required to trace: they were trying to isolate one scent that did not match the scents of the men among whom they lived and worked. And this against an olfactory landscape that was awash with all those other scents, most of them teeming with irritants.

So the dogs sniffed and snuffled. They sneezed. They grew frustrated and anxious. Their nostrils felt like they were being attacked by ants. The animals became fractious and angry and snarled at each other and the handlers when their paths crossed. Their handlers became as frustrated as the dogs, aware that thirty of their comrades and one short-tempered officer were depending on them.

Eventually one of the Alsatians did seem to lock on to something. Its handler felt a nervous tremor of relief stir within him. The dog stiffened. The handler stiffened. The other handler brought his dog across. Both dogs sniffed heartily at the spot. The thirty troopers and the officer watched expectantly.

Then the dogs, with handlers in tow, set off at a gallop towards the forest – which the exasperated officer had already convinced himself was the most likely place anyway, the farmhouse being exonerated. He bellowed at the troopers to follow.

The meadow rang with the sound of thirty bolt-action rifles being cocked ready at the prospect of proper soldierly action instead of playing fire brigades. Thirty pairs of boots pounded towards the trees, followed by the officer and his Luger.

The little white dog was covered in pine needles, bits of twig and sticky burrs. He sat patiently while Charlie picked them off. The dog enjoyed the attention but Charlie also found something soothing in their instant friendship. It was a moment of innocence, the kind of thing people did instead of killing each other. It was a reminder that such a time had once existed. It offered the possibility that it could exist again.

But not just yet, for the dog rose to his feet and stood as stiff as a statue, muscles tensed. His left ear had pricked up and the fur was erect on his back and neck. A low growl sounded deep in his throat. Charlie shushed him and listened hard. After a moment he made out faint noises in the distance, coming from the part of the forest closest to the crash site. Gradually they became identifiable: the crunching and crackling of heavy feet and bodies forcing their way through the forest and in his direction. He could hear the searchers calling to one another – or at least one man who was calling to the others. There were other sounds too, and these were the most worrying of all: the occasional barking of at least two dogs – by the sound of them, not small fellows like his scruffy friend but large beasts, most likely Alsatians.

The little dog had heard enough. He dashed away.

'Very wise,' thought Charlie as he slid back beneath the roots of the oak tree.

He assumed the little dog had gone, but he was wrong. A moment later he heard him growling overhead.

So now they both waited. Not for long.


The two Alsatians and their handlers burst into the clearing, followed closely by the officer.

There, as if waiting for them, was the small white dog. It set up a frenzied barrage of barking, then turned tail and fled, as speedily as it had sprinted from the farmyard and the meadow.

The officer was beside himself with fury. It was clear what had happened. The Alsatians had not been following the trail of the enemy pilot – or of any human being – but that of the stupid little dog. He should have shot the cur.

He shouted for the troopers to turn about. This was a

wild goose chase. Either the English pilot had bailed out, unseen, and by some inexplicable freak of luck the Spitfire had come down in one piece without him, or he had gone to ground elsewhere. In either case he would have to surface sooner or later.

And the officer had an idea how and where and with whom to begin the search for him. For which he would not need any canine assistance.

Charlie listened to the racket taking place only yards from where he lay hidden – men and animals crashing through undergrowth into the clearing, shrill barks that could only be the little dog's, a lot of angry shouting in German, and finally more crashing noises, this time gradually growing fainter as the search party retreated.

Now came silence, dangerous and untrustworthy. Had his pursuers really all departed? Had they posted guards to keep watch in case their quarry might show himself?

So he stayed where he was. He had a hunch he knew who would give him the all-clear.

# 11

On his return to RAF Hawkinge, Henry Banham could not help but be conscious of the glances that came his way as he walked across the base to the operations hut where he had his spartan office. It seemed to him that they were not the usual open, friendly glances; it seemed to him that they had a wary cast to them, evoking in him a feeling of foreboding. They were the kind of glances that came when a sortie went wrong or when an aircraft, or several, failed to return from a mission.

But no, that could not be the case today. His flight was flying no sorties today, which was precisely why he had taken the opportunity to slip off to London. And now, as far as he could see, the base was going about its business much as normal, with no evidence of a scramble or anything untoward. He heard the roar of aircraft taking off and paused to watch half a dozen Spitfires, none of them from his flight, lift into the sky and swing towards the coast and France. No siren was sounding to warn of incoming enemy aircraft, so it was just a sortie setting out, another sweep over the Pas-de-Calais to keep Göring's Luftwaffe vermin down. Regular culling, the only way.

Henry shook his misgivings aside. Those glances – he was imagining things. He was out of sorts after the dispiriting information he had received in Harley

Street, that was all. Or the heat and the muggy drive back to Kent had got the better of him. He was worrying over nothing. The glances were for no more sinister reason than the fact that he was wearing civilian clothes – though without the fedora – and civilians were a rare species on the base. The glances were merely glances of curiosity. Yes, that was the explanation.

No, it was not.

Corporal Edwardes was waiting for him outside his office. He looked nervous. He saluted as Henry approached.

'Sorry to waylay you, sir. The gate phoned to say you'd arrived. I'd asked them to let me know immediately.'

Henry unlocked the office and entered. He loosened his tie.

'Well, here I am. What's so urgent?'

'There's a problem, sir. Charlie Quinn, sir.'

Henry turned to face the corporal.

'We don't know where he is, sir.'

'He's on rotation rest today. All the pilots in my flight are. You know that. He'll be having a drink in The Cat.'

'No, I mean him and his aircraft, sir. Gone, sir.'

Henry felt a knot form in his stomach. Those wary glances: not his imagination, then; not worrying over nothing. Damnation.

Edwardes cleared his throat. 'He told his fitter and rigger to get his Spitfire fuelled and ready. Told them there was some problem he wanted to check, said he had to take the aircraft up to do it. They did as he said and off he went. Chose a time when no sorties were going out. The tower only had contact with him during and immediately after take-off. Nothing thereafter. They tried, but he didn't acknowledge or respond.'

'Radio silence,' muttered Henry, to himself as much as to Edwardes.

'He was tracked going out over the Channel at Folkestone. Lost him after that, sir. Fact is, we have no idea where he went or where he is now.'

'Was there really a problem with the Spitfire?'

'His ground crew think not.'

'So what are you actually telling me, Edwardes?'

The corporal cleared his throat again. 'Some of the pilots are saying he's gone on a sortie, sir. An independent one, sort of. He had a full load of ammunition.'

Henry removed his jacket. 'Independent sortie? Do you mean unauthorised? Ludicrous idea.'

The difficulty was, with Charlie Quinn it was not ludicrous.

Henry hung the jacket on the hook behind the door. The knot in his stomach had grown larger and tighter. His thoughts returned to Harley Street. There was another worry that was nagging him. He looked at Edwardes.

'You've only said about Charlie. This independent sortie – you're not telling me he's gone out alone?'

'Afraid so, sir. No wingman. And he's out of flying time by now. Out of fuel.'

No wingman. Insane, quite insane.

'Check with other bases. Maybe he circled back but couldn't make it as far as Hawkinge, maybe he had to put down somewhere else. Maybe the ground crew's mistaken and there actually is a problem with the aircraft.'

'We've already been in touch with over a dozen bases so far, sir. Bomber Command as well as Fighter, anything with a runway. Nothing, sir – he hasn't landed, hasn't contacted any of them. We're still checking, but frankly, sir, I'm not holding my breath.'

Henry turned to gaze out of the window. 'Then you're suggesting he's gone down somewhere. Shot down or crashed. Dead or in enemy hands. Or ditched in the Channel. At best stranded somewhere.'

'Not my place to suggest anything, sir. Just putting you in the picture is all.'

'Which is what I need to do for Percy. And post-haste.'

Percy Kingdom was Henry's squadron leader. But Henry would have no need to leave his office to put him in the picture. As he spoke there was a rap on the open door. He turned to see Kingdom standing there. The squadron leader did not look happy.

'Thank you, Edwardes,' said Henry. 'That'll be all.'

Edwardes saluted and hurried away, looking glad to be doing so. Kingdom closed the door after him.

'Henry, what the blazes is going on? What's this nonsense I've just heard about Charlie Quinn? Tell me it's not true.'

Henry sighed. 'Wish I could, Percy.'

He motioned for Kingdom to sit in one of the two upright chairs. He took the other one. He clasped his hands together, his long fingers flexing up and down like bony wings, then unclasped the hands and brought them to rest on the curved arms of the chair.

'Percy, there's something I need to tell you. About Charlie Quinn …'

# 12

The Destry farmhouse was a mess. Even Philippe, who had been expecting the worst, was shocked. Wherever he looked he saw the wanton and spiteful destruction that men committed when they were driven by contempt. Every room was a disaster, the family's few sticks of furniture overturned and broken, everything tossed about in every direction, clothes strewn everywhere and trampled underfoot, every bed upended, every cupboard emptied of its contents, crockery dashed to the stone floor and smashed. Josette's ill-fated butter churn had been overturned again, this time crushed beyond repair by German boots, which meant no butter for the family; more worryingly, it also meant none for the loathed ravitaillement men, the Germans' requisition collectors; it was never wise for the Destry farm to fall short and attract their attention.

Josette clawed at her hair and clothes in dismay. The air was blue with Pépé's imprecations and blasphemies. Albert shook his head sorrowfully. He was close to tears as he turned to Philippe.

'How long do we have to put up with these animals?'

Pépé overheard him.

'Albert, you're a fool,' he said flatly. 'This is how our lives will be from now on. Get used to it. You call them animals, but to the Boche it's us who are the animals. Our only uses are as slave labour and to produce food for their bellies. Don't say I didn't warn you. The last time we had to deal with these scum I was older than you are now but I still did my duty. I was an honest poilu, I marched off to the front, I rotted in the trenches with my comrades, I dodged bullets and swallowed my share of poison gas. Whereas you, you're not only a fool, Albert, you're a coward too. You and your brother. If either of you were man enough to do your duty like I did mine –'

'We did our duty, Pépé. We did our military service. But when this war came I had a farm to run and Philippe had his patients. Would you rather the farm went to ruin and the people of Auny had no doctor? Heh?'

'I'm not talking about last year, when the Boche overran our feeble army. I'm talking about now. Why don't you do something now? Why don't you stand up for our country? Do something, in the name of God!'

But Josette, who had sat herself on the raised hearthstone at the corner of the fireplace and was inspecting her injured foot, had other ideas. She turned her tear-streaked face to her husband. Her eyes blazed.

'Don't you dare, Albert Destry,' she snapped. 'There's this farm to run and no end of work to do. The cows won't milk themselves, the hay doesn't cut itself and jump up as haystacks, and the last time I looked the hens weren't collecting their own eggs. There's your family to look after and feed, including that geriatric fool of a father. You're a farmer, not a fighter. So pay no heed to him. You've got us into enough trouble already.'

'How have I got us into trouble?' protested Alert. 'I've done nothing.'

'Precisely,' agreed Pépé triumphantly.

Albert ran his fingers despairingly through his hair, looked helplessly from his father to his wife and back to his father again, seemed to be trying to formulate a reply of some kind, but then, apparently defeated in that aspiration, turned on his heel and went outside.

'Papa!' called Fernand.

Philippe sent his father and his sister-in-law a black look, to which both were oblivious, and followed his brother out to the yard.

'Philippe – what about my foot?' Josette called after him.


'Battle fatigue? Quinn?' said Percy Kingdom, echoing what Henry had just told him. 'What utter rot, Henry. You're not serious?'

Kingdom was a big man, tall and broad. It was a wonder he could fit himself into the cockpit of a Spitfire. Henry was glad that he had invited him to sit down; on his feet, the squadron leader could be an intimidating presence.

Kingdom produced his Dunhill briar pipe and leather tobacco pouch. The tobacco also came from the Dunhill shop on London's Duke Street. It was rumoured to be the same blend as that supplied to the king – no one but the king was supposed to have it, but Percy Kingdom had ways of getting what he wanted.

Henry pushed an ashtray across the desk.

'Use another term if you prefer, Percy,' he said.

'Combat exhaustion, burn-out, nervous collapse. It's been recognised in one form or another for thousands of years – the author of the Book of Deuteronomy knew of it.'

'Pardon my biblical ignorance. What about calling it good old-fashioned weakness?'

Henry folded his thin hands together and gazed down at them. He had known this would not be easy. Motoring back to Hawkinge he had turned over in his mind a score of ways to tackle Kingdom, ways in which to explain the Harley Street doctor's diagnosis of what was wrong with Charlie Quinn. Ways in which to convince the prickly squadron leader that his best pilot needed urgent help.

He had known it would not be easy but what he had not bargained for was that he would be too late, that even before he could straighten matters with Kingdom, Charlie would have done the rashest thing, the most insane thing conceivable.

Henry checked himself. 'Insane': twice now he had used that description. Not helpful in this context.

But it was as if Kingdom had sensed the notion in the air. He glanced up from the pipe.

'Or are you saying he's off his rocker, Henry?'

'It's not weakness and he's not off his rocker. Look at his record. A dozen kills, probably more, considering he's chalked up twice as many probables. Gazetted twice – DSO and DFC. Is that the record of a weak man?'

'I know his record as well as you do. So, he's not weak. Slipped a cog, then. Screw loose. It happens.'

'Not that either. Not in Charlie's case.'

'I'm damned if I can see an alternative explanation. Weak or gaga – which is it, Henry?'

'Percy, we send boys barely out of their teens hurtling through the air four miles up at four hundred miles an hour in a machine with no more elbow room than a motorcycle sidecar. We show them how to kill by pushing a button. They think it's a doddle until they realise the enemy only has to push a button too. We expect them to make decisions in a fraction of a second. Get it right, they live until the next scrap; get it wrong, they're just a name in a telegram. They're in dogfights with so many aircraft spinning about like dodgem cars it's a miracle they don't ram each other, friend or foe. They have an average life expectancy counted in weeks – any man with as much experience as Charlie Quinn knows he's living on borrowed time. We expect them to keep this up day after day as if they're taking the seven-forty from Esher to the City. So you tell me, Percy, who's gaga – us or them?'

Henry sat back in the chair, taken aback by his own monologue. He worried that he might have gone too far.

But Kingdom seemed unfazed. He continued calmly packing tobacco into the bowl of the pipe.

'We got through it, Henry, you and I and others like us,' he said. 'Still do. Every time we lead our flights, we share what's facing them. Why haven't you buckled? Why haven't I? Why hasn't everyone in the service? We manage, so why make an exception for Charlie Quinn?'

He struck a match and put it to the pipe. For a few moments he said nothing as he got it under way.

Henry waited.

But when Kingdom spoke again it was as if he had ignited an anger within himself.

'What would you have us do, Henry? Stand our pilots down and feed them cocoa and ask Nursey to tuck them in every time they get the collywobbles? Quinn's probably dead anyway. Why are we even talking about this?'

Henry went to the window. Another sortie was preparing to leave. There was the familiar chorus of coughs as the Merlin engines kicked into life, followed by the roar that built to a crescendo as the pilots – so young, he reminded himself – gunned them ready for take-off.

Sometimes, he reflected, Percy Kingdom was like one of those Merlin engines: croaky and complaining to start with, but once he got going there was no holding him. He had to be allowed to warm up in his own time.

So Henry said nothing, leaving him all the space he needed. Behind him Kingdom puffed away in silence. Then Henry heard the pipe being set down in the ashtray.

'I once heard Churchill holding forth about psychiatrists,' said Kingdom. 'There was this dinner party Clara's father laid on. I didn't want to be there – knee deep in politicians – but she wouldn't let me off.'

Henry recalled that Kingdom's father-in-law owned a string of regional newspapers; not so many nor so large as to make him a Beaverbrook, but important enough in the febrile world of politics.

'Churchill was there. The conversation turned to

exactly what you're talking about – the effect of war on people's minds. They were talking about civilians initially, what the Blitz had done to people mentally as well as physically and materially. Then the discussion turned to our fighting forces – shell shock as it was called in the last debacle, that kind of thing, whether it should be allowed as a genuine medical condition.'

'I see,' said Henry uncertainly.

'Churchill was in no doubt, of course. Psychiatrists are a scourge, he said, charlatans, hangers-on. We should be restricting the work of "these gentlemen", as he called them, as much as possible. Someone asked why. "Because their questions only serve to disturb large numbers of healthy normal men and women," he said.'

Henry grunted unhappily but said nothing. If the battle was lost, it was lost. No point rising to Percy's bait.

But it turned out not to be bait at all. Kingdom had warmed up. He was ready for take-off.

'Struck me as a bit off-kilter, that,' he said. 'A bit rich, coming from someone with a temperament like Churchill's, who drinks like a fish and is pretty well permanently three sheets to the wind – that night being no exception – who insults anybody and everybody for no good reason – again, that night was typical – and who is beyond any question the most arrogant human being I've ever met in my life. And he's standing there like a maharaja, loving that his words are being lapped up by a roomful of sycophants.'

Henry was intrigued. 'I thought you liked Churchill.'

'You've never heard me say that, Henry. I consider

him exactly the right man to get us through this present scrape. Different thing entirely. Beyond that I wouldn't give him the time of day. And the best of it is, he has what he calls his black dog days. Did you know that? Bad show.'

'I didn't know.' Henry frowned. 'What's your point, Percy?'

'Only that Churchill's a fine one to rail against psychiatrists, with those black dog days of his. The beam in thine own eye and all that, since we're being biblical. Now, this Harley Street man, tell me what he says about Charlie Quinn.'

Henry looked askance at his squadron leader. 'I tried to, and you bit my head off.'

Kingdom picked up the pipe and gazed reflectively into its bowl. 'That was before I remembered about Churchill. Great leader but the man's a hypocrite. I don't want to be a hypocrite.' He put the pipe back in his mouth. 'So tell me again. I'm listening.'

Henry cautiously resumed his seat.

# 13

Philippe found his brother standing in the middle of the yard, beside the three German trucks.

'Pépé's old, Albert. Half the time he doesn't even understand what he's saying. You know that. Don't let him get to you.'

Albert continued staring at the trucks. 'Easy for you to say. You don't live with him. I have to put up with his jibes and whinges every day.'

Philippe said nothing. Behind him a door slammed. Fernand appeared.

'Pépé's still ranting,' he said. 'Papa, why don't you just tell him what you do, you and Uncle Philippe?'

Albert kicked the tyre of a truck and rounded on him. 'And exactly what do you think we do anyway, young man?'

Fernand looked uncertain, shaken by his father's tone. 'You fight for France.'

'You think so? You think we fight? Truly? I wonder.'

Philippe gently touched his brother's arm, to restrain any further words, lest they be regretted later, or any more fractious show of temper or frustration. He turned to his nephew.

'We do what we can, Fernand. Yes, we see it as fighting for France, but perhaps not in the way you think. Pépé probably wouldn't consider it enough. We don't fight with guns or bombs.'

The boy looked puzzled.

Philippe nodded towards the trucks. 'We won't be blowing these up, for example – we wouldn't know how to. We won't shoot at the Germans, whatever they do to us – we don't have guns. Your father doesn't even have his shotgun, not since the Germans called for all guns to be handed in. And even if we were able to do those things, we couldn't – we wouldn't want to. I'm a doctor, Fernand, I try to heal people, not harm them. Your father has never lifted his hand in anger to anyone.' He smiled at the boy. 'Not even you, though there were times when you deserved it.'

Fernand looked from one man to the other. 'Then what do you do?' He lowered his voice to a whisper. 'What about the men I saw in the barn?'

'Too many questions, Fernand,' said his father.

'Perhaps you'll find out,' Philippe told the boy.

Fernand eyes brightened. 'The English pilot? You're saying you'll help him?'

'I'm not saying anything, Fernand. The question might not even arise. The Germans might have caught him by now.'

'I suppose.'

Philippe turned to Albert. 'I was with Bernard earlier.'

'Yes?'

'Still his same old chorus of hopes and promises about resistance – "Any day now the people of France will rise up." Well, you know how he is.'

'You told him nothing, heh?'

'Of course not. Just the usual nonsense. He has his

84

nonsense that he reels out, I have mine. He's worried about his son, of course. Still no news.'

Albert nodded. He put his arm about Fernand's shoulder. 'Remember you promised you wouldn't say anything to Maman or Pépé?'

'Of course, Papa. I won't say anything to anybody at all.'

'Above all, say nothing to Bernard. He has the biggest mouth in Auny.'

'I won't. I never know if he's drunk or sober.'

'Assume drunk. A safe bet. Now, let's see what our German friends are up to.'

The three of them went to the end of the yard. The Spitfire had been abandoned, with not a trooper in sight.

'They're still in the forest,' said Fernand morosely. 'Still searching.'

'With their hounds of Hades,' said Philippe.

But just then they saw movement in the trees at the edge of the forest. A batch of troopers emerged. They were trudging wearily now, rifles slung on their shoulders, not stomping along or looking their usual bellicose and cocky selves. Then came a further group, just as crestfallen. Then came the two dog handlers with their charges. The Alsatians were no longer straining at their chains; they seemed subdued, almost cowed, heads and tails down, a far cry from their previous demeanour. From time to time they looked up at their handlers, as if seeking reassurance. But all they received was a sharp word of reprimand and a hefty tug on their chains.

Then at the very end of the woebegone caravan came

the officer. He still carried his Luger, but with less gusto than before. He seemed as dejected as the Alsatians.

'There's no prisoner, they've found no one,' declared Fernand, relief and hope mingling in his voice.

'It looks that way,' agreed his father.

'You know what?' said Philippe, in whose breast a tiny flame of hope had begun to reawaken; he had thought it quashed forever.

'What?' said Albert.

'I think I'd better do something about Josette's foot. Just in case things get busy for us later.'

'Hmm,' said Albert.

'Yes, Uncle, yes,' said Fernand. 'Do that.'

'I wonder what's become of Eiffel,' said Albert.

'Hmm,' said Philippe.

Eiffel was having a fine old time. He had intoxicating scents in his nostrils and the world of the forest and the open countryside at his feet. No reasonable dog could ask for more.

He had reached familiar territory, tracks and paths that he recognised, and he was following a route that would bring him back to the farmhouse and his master. All danger was far behind him and he was jogging comfortably along.

He knew nothing of war and armies, had no understanding of nationhood or borders or acts of occupation. He had only his instincts, but they were finely tuned. He knew the humans he liked and trusted, and those from whom he shied away. He accompanied his master as he went about his work, and although he did not understand that work – indeed, he had no concept of work – he knew that there were humans who needed his master and that his master was able to help them and was always ready and willing to do so.

So he loped along, a dog with a mission, a dog who had found someone who needed his master's help.

# 14

Henry Banham took a deep breath. So Percy Kingdom had decided not to be a hypocrite. He wanted to understand about Charlie Quinn.

Fair enough. This was good progress.

'It's difficult for all of us,' Henry began. 'You're right, Percy. But certain things make Charlie's situation different. Because he's our best pilot, with the highest kill tally in the squadron, the others look to him. Primus inter pares, first among equals – that's a weighty burden.'

A puff of smoke from the pipe. 'Seems to me he thrives on it.'

'Hear me out. Then there's the tally itself. It's not a cricket score sheet. Every mark is a life that Charlie has taken. A young life, someone like himself, with a wife and maybe children too. That's a long list of lives destroyed – wives, children, mothers, fathers, sisters, brothers. Not an easy thing for a young man to have on his conscience.'

Another cloud of smoke. 'We're at war, Henry.'

'Don't pretend those same thoughts don't come to you in the lonely watches of the night. I remind you, Percy – you said you'd listen.'

Kingdom raised an apologetic hand.

'The third factor is guilt.'

'Isn't that what you've just been describing?'

'This is guilt of a different kind. My man in Harley Street calls it survivor guilt. In Charlie's case it's to do with the death of Tim Kemp.'

'His wingman. Killed last month.'

Henry nodded. 'We both know the responsibility a lead pilot feels towards his wingman. Kemp was Charlie's wingman from the very start, from Battle of Britain days.'

'Obviously his death has hit Quinn hard. But we all have people we mourn.'

'This is more complicated. It comes from the manner of Kemp's death. Charlie feels personally responsible and guilty that he himself survived. You know the facts – three large enemy formations on course for the English coast that day, over a hundred aircraft – Stukas, Ju 88s and an escort of 109s. We threw everything at them. Eight squadrons went up. Charlie came home, many others didn't, including Kemp. But Charlie was convinced that Kemp could have bailed out after he was hit. Instead he rammed one of the 109s as it was closing on Charlie. Kemp's ammo was gone, so he used the only weapon he had – his own aircraft.'

'I read Quinn's report. Didn't agree with it then, still don't. Kemp's aircraft was simply out of control – the collision was accidental.'

Henry drummed his fingers briefly on the arm of the chair. 'We'll never know what the truth is. But it doesn't matter. As my man in Harley Street puts it, all that actually matters is what Charlie himself believes. The collision scattered the other 109s and gave him the chance to get into cloud and lose them. The way he sees it, he's alive today only because Kemp sacrificed himself.'

Kingdom removed the pipe from his mouth and studied its bowl. He began poking at it with a dead match. 'So you sent Quinn to your man in Harley Street. Don't you think you should have checked with me first?'

'We were in uncharted territory. Charlie was behaving erratically – falling out with other pilots, never satisfied with any wingman he took on to replace Kemp. Frankly he'd become a pain, a disruptive influence. He even spoke about operating solo. I didn't want to log anything formally about his condition until I at least knew what that condition might actually be, and I certainly didn't want to involve you or a service medic. It would have become official – why put something like that on a man's record before we understand it and know whether it can be resolved? My plan was to brief you today, tell you I'd be taking Charlie off active duties for a while. He wouldn't have liked it but I didn't intend to give him a choice. He'd be flying a desk while receiving treatment – and if you agreed, preferably in Harley Street with my man, who's offered to waive his fee.'

'Generous of him, but that won't happen now.'

'No, it won't. As you pointed out, Charlie may be dead.'

Kingdom sighed. 'Next of kin?'

'Wife and child.'

'I'll let the Air Ministry know. They'll do the necessary. His wife will have the telegram today.'

Henry thought this over. Just a name in a telegram.

90

In his mind's eye he saw Émilie receiving the telegram.

'Don't do that,' he told Kingdom. 'I'll tell her myself, in person. Better that way.'

'As you wish,' shrugged Kingdom. 'Missing,' he added, his thoughts perhaps following a similar course to Henry's. 'He's only missing, that's all. At this stage anyway. His wife must hold on to that.'

He finished the business with the pipe, clamped it back between his teeth, then puffed for a moment until he was content all was well with it.

'Missing, yes,' he mused again. 'Enough for now.'

'Bad enough,' said Henry.

# 15

'It's all right now, Charlie,' said the voice for which he had been waiting. 'The Germans have gone.'

Charlie inched his way out from his hiding place. It was a slow process, his left arm tormented by spasms of pain with every jarring movement. It had become worse during his confinement.

The stranger observed him from the shadow of the pines, his expression as bland and impassive as ever. No trace of sympathy in his gaze, no indication of any concern.

Charlie rose cautiously to his feet. 'This arm – I have to do something about it.'

'No. I told you. Just wait. It's better if you wait.'

Another spasm struck. 'Wait for what? For it to fester and drop off?'

The man stuck his hands in his pockets and leant back against a pine tree. He seemed perfectly at ease.

'That photo of your family, I couldn't help but look at it. Your wife's very beautiful, if you'll allow me to say so. What's her name? Your child – a boy, I think. Yes, a boy, you have a son.'

The throb in Charlie's head doubled in ferocity. It brought a wave of dizziness. He steadied himself against the oak. Had he really begun to trust this man who told him nothing he wanted to know but thought nothing of poking his nose into his life as if it was his right?

'My family is none of your business.'

'We'll get you home to them, Charlie. Don't worry.'

Getting home. Those words again. And this time it was as if Charlie's final defences had been breached. The throb in his head, the pain in his arm, but above all the vividness with which Émilie and his son were now here in his mind, no longer frozen in the grey tones of the photograph that he had refused to allow himself to look at for fear of its effect on him, but now here before him and so real that he could have touched them, could have smelt them, felt the warmth of their skin and their breath on his cheek – all these things seemed to come together and wring the last shreds of defiance from him.

'My wife is called Émilie.'

It hurt to speak her name and to hear it as he said it. Yet saying it and hearing it were what he wanted. The statement came out only as a whisper but the man heard. Just as he seemed to hear everything, spoken or not.

'Beautiful name,' he replied. He repeated it. 'Émilie.'

'It's French. My wife is French.'

'All the more reason for you to hate the Germans, then, considering what they've done to her country.'

'I don't hate them.'

'No?'

'No.'

'You kill them, though.'

'Only because I have to, and because I know that if I don't, they'll kill me. Doesn't mean I hate them.'

93

'You surprise me.'

'Be surprised all you want. They're my enemies, I hate what they do and what they stand for, I hate what they've done, I hate what they'll continue to do if we don't stop them – but I don't hate *them*. I'm supposed to regard them as vermin but I can't manage that either.'

He forgot the stranger's presence for a moment and wondered instead what Henry Banham would make of his confession. On second thoughts, no need to wonder; he knew exactly what Henry would make of it.

As for the stranger, he remained resolutely silent, making no comment, offering no judgement, just waiting for whatever else Charlie had to say and watching from those unfathomable eyes that always seemed to be appraising him, sizing him up.

Charlie thought about the other things he had never told Henry. Many other things, buried deep within him. It was not only Henry who had never heard him speak of them, for he had never spoken of them to anyone, never admitted them, never shared them. Never with any other flyer. Nor with Émilie. Above all, never with Émilie.

But there seemed to be no stopping him now. Perhaps the stranger had known that all that was needed was silence at just the right moment. Perhaps he knew that in the clamour of war it was silence, only silence, that could unlock what was in a man's heart.

'These enemies of mine,' Charlie said, so quietly that he could have been speaking to himself, 'I see them face-to-face sometimes. Odd thing, to look a man in the eye when you're out to kill each other. Our aircraft pass very close sometimes – that's how it is up there, swirling about in all directions – then it happens and our paths cross. There might be less than the width of a room between us. We glance at one another the way you'd glance at someone as you pass them in the street or on the road in your motor car – there's only time for the quickest of glances but in that glance you see so much. Just for that split second I see my enemy, then he's gone.'

Now the stranger chose to speak. 'And what is it that you see?'

'That he's exactly like me, this enemy, this man I have to kill. There's never any hatred in his eyes, or if there is I can't see it, only fear. I don't know if it's the same for him when he looks at me. Can he tell that I'm as afraid as he is? That I don't hate him? That I don't want to kill him but I don't want to die either and that's why I'll kill him if I can? It's the only reason I have for killing him, in fact. The only reason – no other. And I wonder what kind of man he is. Is he a good man? Does he love someone? Is he loved in return? Who frets about him, who's waiting for him at home? Who'll weep if I kill him today? Because, make no mistake, I will kill him if I can. That's what I see, questions like these. If there was a way for us to stop, I honestly believe that's what we'd do, both of us. But there's no such way. My questions can't be answered and we carry on until one of us is shot down. Killed, as like as not.'

'But not you. You haven't been killed.'

'Not yet anyway. Came close this time.'

95

'Did you see the man who shot you down today?'

Charlie shook his head, ignoring the stab of pain. 'No. Today wasn't one of those days. Today was ... different. But I don't hate him for what he did – that stays the same.'

He studied his hands, fingers extended. The hands were trembling, both of them, so the tremble was nothing to do with his injury. Why would they not stop trembling?

'We're the same, my enemy and I. We get up in the morning, he in his world, I in mine, but we're just the same. We do the same things – we wash, eat, get dressed. We go from home or base leaving things undone – the book not yet read, the fence we said we'd repair, the disagreement with a loved one – believing we'll return to them, complete them, set things right. There'll be time, we believe. No one closes his door behind him believing he'll never open it again. If I could see my enemy this morning as he sets out, if I could see what he's left undone, could I still kill him?'

He looked at his hands again. They continued to tremble.

'These hands kill. They take life.'

'They also give life, Charlie. They hold your son. They give love. They protect. You'd do anything to protect your son.'

'Any father would.'

'All men are sons but only the most fortunate are fathers. Fathers protect. That's their duty, above everything else. You haven't told me your son's name.'

The trembling grew worse. 'Same as mine – he's

called Charlie.'

He could hear Émilie saying it. *Sharr-lee*. That echo in his mind both hurt and comforted him as much as saying Émilie's name had done. He allowed his eyes to close. And here they were again, right here before him, Émilie and little Charlie. So close.

He opened his eyes. To his surprise the man was smiling. It was the only time he had ever done so.

'You named your son Charlie,' he said. 'Like you.'

'It's a family tradition – the first boy is always called Charlie.'

'So your father's name was Charlie too.'

'Yes.'

'Tell me about him.'

Charlie shrugged absently, his thoughts still on Émilie and his son. 'Nothing to tell. I never knew him.'

'How sad.'

Then a curtain seemed to descend in Charlie's mind. He looked directly at the stranger, peered through the woodland shadows and brought him properly into focus.

'My father is none of your damned business either.'

# 16

The German officer was now having a busy and much more satisfying afternoon. Busy, because he had a list and he was working his way steadily through it. Satisfying, partly because he was an orderly man and ticking things off lists pleased him, and partly because he was doing what he enjoyed even more than he enjoyed lists: he was pushing people around.

All this without a single Alsatian dog in sight. Nor any wooden-headed troopers sniggering or getting in his way. Always better to work alone. A valuable lesson.

His list comprised the names of eleven families, all of them residents of Auny-sous-Bois. They were families who had at least one man – a son, a father, a brother – serving indefinite time as a prisoner of war in Germany, working as forced labour in a Stalag camp or in a factory, a coal or ore mine, or, in rare and fortunate cases, on a farm.

The families were of course forbidden to know the whereabouts of their menfolk. But he knew where they were. He had a list detailing that, too. He also knew the work to which each was assigned – another list. Most importantly, he could arrange for any of them to be reassigned to alternative work, for better or worse, depending on the cooperation he received from their family in response to the demands he made of them.

In short, he had power – enough to secure him spies and informers in every village street and bar and behind every hedgerow and gatepost.

The garage owner was ninth on his list. The officer found him bent over the engine of a rusty old Citroën, an open bottle of wine by his feet. No drinking glass to be seen, just the bottle.

The officer picked it up and examined it.

'So, what do you have for me?' he said.

Bernard straightened up, rubbing his back. He looked frightened. 'Nothing yet. I'm trying my best.'

'Not good enough.'

The officer held the bottle beneath his nose to assess the bouquet. It was foul, almost as bad as the steamy fragrance from the nearby septic tank.

'Do you drink this or clean engines with it? I hope you didn't pay black market prices for it.'

'How can I give you information if there's none to tell you?'

The officer walked slowly around the car, one hand in his pocket, the other holding the bottle.

'The Kommando boss at the coal mine where your son is assigned reports that your lad won't last much longer. He's not used to mining work.' The officer lowered his voice. 'I'll bend a rule, I'll tell you where the mine is. It's in the Ruhr. The mines there are the very worst, the very toughest, believe me. The bosscs are particularly vicious.' He smiled brightly. 'Have you ever been down a coal mine?'

'Of course not.'

'You can't imagine what hell it is – a kilometre underground, you can't breathe, the dust rots your lungs. You work on your hands and knees, swinging a pick at solid rock to get to the seam, constant danger of an explosion or being crushed to death if the tunnel caves in. They often do, by the way. Your son belongs in the open air.'

'I know.'

'I could see to it that he's posted to a healthy farm in Saxony. They're homely types in Saxony. Not like Kommando bosses. But whether he gets such a posting, that's in your hands. If he doesn't, it's anybody's guess which will happen first – will he die or will I lose patience with you? Better if he dies, because if I lose patience I'll make sure his death comes even harder. A shame too – he'd enjoy Saxony.'

'Please. There's someone I suspect. But I can't get him to admit anything or give anything away. Not yet. Doesn't even want petrol coupons.'

'The doctor? Him again? I'm fed up hearing about him. I don't believe he's up to anything. He's an old woman.'

'He's the kind of bourgeois intellectual who'd be involved in getting a resistance movement going – his type is always at the forefront of trouble. His brother would follow suit. Haven't you heard their father shooting his mouth off? He's no friend to Germany. Like father, like sons. With my help you'd have all of them.'

The officer was mindful of his fruitless search of the Destry farm.

'Get me something tangible,' he said. 'If I interrogated everyone that you and your fellow countrymen accuse, I'd do nothing else all day. Do you know how many letters of denunciation we receive each week? Dozens, in this area alone. All anonymous, of course, all without evidence. You French have made poison pen letters a national pastime – opportunities to settle old scores. I won't waste my time on your doctor or his brother or their idiot father unless I can stop whatever they're up to – if they're up to anything. Someone else would simply take over from them. I need comprehensive intelligence. If they're printing anti-Reich propaganda, where's the printing press? Where do they store the paper? Who supplies it? Who distributes the finished material? If they're planning violent action, where do they hide their weapons? Where did they acquire them? Find out who else is working with them, then I can round up the whole nest. Are you sober enough to understand?'

'Arrest them, interrogate them and you'll get all that information from their own mouths. Won't need my help.'

'If you don't like my terms, we can terminate our arrangement. It would mean the end of the line for your son. You want that?'

The garage owner shook his head unhappily.

'Now, a change of subject. This enemy aircraft that came down earlier today –'

'What enemy aircraft?'

'You're stupid and drunk but you're not deaf and blind. It looks like the pilot survived the crash. He needs somewhere to hide and someone to help him. You're going to find out who that is.'

'How can I do that?'

'I don't care. You have twenty-four hours to tell me where he is and who's hiding him. Do that and I'll leave things as they are for your son. He'll still be in the coal mine and you can still make things better for him. Business as usual for you and me. But this matter of the enemy pilot, let me down on that and I'll have your son's shifts doubled and his food ration cut in half. That's fair, isn't it?'

He handed the bottle back.

'Prost!' he said cheerily.

Then he climbed into his small open-topped jeep – known to every German soldier as a Kübelwagen, as tinny and basic as the bucket in its name – and rattled off to bully the next unfortunate on his list.

Eiffel was insistent. He stood four-square before Philippe in the yard, barking at his master. Whatever Philippe tried to do to calm him down, even scratching the little dog's ears, the barking continued. Eiffel simply bounced away, resumed his determined stance and barked again. He shot forward and nipped at his master's feet, then growled, his paws scrabbling at the concrete as he tried to make Philippe move.

Philippe ran his hand over his shiny head as he watched the dog's antics.

'He's trying to tell me something. He wants me to go with him.' He paused. 'Could be he's found something.'

'Or someone,' said Fernand.

'Don't get your hopes up,' cautioned Albert.

The brothers and the boy looked at one another. No

one dared articulate the thought in all their minds.

'I need to go and see,' said Philippe.

'You should, heh,' agreed Albert.

'Hurry, Uncle.'

Philippe snapped his cycle clips in place and crossed the yard to fetch his bicycle. But Eiffel had other ideas. He scooted into the farmhouse and resumed barking there. Philippe heard Pépé swearing and Josette shouting at the dog to shut up. She called for Philippe.

He went indoors. Eiffel was dashing back and forth across the floor, his nails clacking on the stone flags. In the corner was Philippe's medical bag, left there after he had tended to Josette's foot. Eiffel was bounding up to the bag, barking at it, then racing back towards the door. When Philippe entered, the dog ran up to him and then back to the bag. Only when Philippe picked the bag up did Eiffel stop barking.

'Silence is golden,' said Josette. 'What use is that animal, Philippe? Find yourself a good wife instead. You really should.'

'Good idea, Josette. I hear there's a lot to be said for a good wife.'

He returned outside, exchanged a long look with his brother, then strapped the bag in its usual place on the rear pannier and cycled off in pursuit of Eiffel.

Charlie was feeling nauseous. Any moment now he would throw up. The dizziness had returned. This time it would not go away. His vision swam, everything was out of focus. His sense of balance seemed to have gone as well; he staggered and had to grab at the oak tree for support.

He should never have complied with the stranger's advice to leave the arm alone, for he had no doubt that it was to blame – blood poisoning or similar had set in. He should have opened the wound and dug the shrapnel out and to hell with the consequences.

Meanwhile the stranger had performed one of his vanishing tricks and was nowhere to be seen. How did he manage to slip away like that unnoticed?

Charlie made his way to the stream. He should have drunk more water through the afternoon; dehydration was probably part of the problem. Now he guzzled down several handfuls, only stopping when bile rose in his throat, acidic and sour. He vomited; the content was all water. His eyes filled with tears. He waited until the retching stopped, then wiped his eyes and unsheathed the knife again. He had no means of sterilising it, but too bad; after all, he could hardly make matters any worse. He still had the tremble and he wondered if he would be able to handle the knife accurately, what with that and the fuzziness of his vision.

But before he could find out, a rustle in the undergrowth told him he had company.

# 17

Philippe cycled as far as he could after Eiffel into the forest, but there came the time when the tracks ran out and the going became impossible by bicycle.

He dismounted and took in his surroundings. He was in a part of the forest that was unknown to him, deeper in its interior than he ever had reason to go previously. But something about it seemed wrong, seemed not as it should be. It took him a few moments to work out what it was. Then he realised.

The German search party had come through here. The evidence was everywhere – at least for a man who knew woodland. He saw where the bed of pine needles and cones that constituted the forest floor had been churned by many feet. He saw where ferns and brush had been trampled down. He saw thin, freshly snapped pine boughs still attached to their trees, the bark split and the fleshy wood where they had been bent to breaking point still white and soft. It was with no sense of surprise that he saw a pile of recent dog turds, large specimens such as could be expected from an Alsatian.

But if the Germans had come this far, or further perhaps, how could Eiffel be leading him to someone that they had failed to find? Perhaps the dog was mistaken. But no, that was unfair. All Eiffel had done was all a dog could ever do – bark. It was his master who would be in error, who had misinterpreted his message.

And here was Eiffel again, as importunate as before, yelping to urge him onward.

'Yes, Eiffel. Yes, yes. I'm coming.'

Philippe sighed and set the bicycle down. Master and dog together now on foot: so be it. He took the medical bag and picked his way between the trees, looking for the small scrap of white ahead of him that was Eiffel.

The dog never faltered, however deep they went. His technique was to race ahead, then double back to check that his master was still following, perhaps also to tell him to get a move on; then off he dashed again. A dozen times he was lost from view, hidden among the trees and ferny undergrowth, a dozen times he came bouncing back, as eager as ever to get on with his mission.

Then came the moment that ensured his master would never doubt him again.

Philippe had stepped into a small glade. All around were the usual tall pines but here there were birches as well and one great oak tree. A tiny stream trickled through the glade, hidden underground elsewhere.

The man was standing by the stream. He was young, in his twenties, and wearing what was unmistakably an RAF uniform, although it was grubby and torn. He was pointing a pistol directly at Philippe. Eiffel was sitting by the man's feet, scratching himself happily, with apparently not a concern in the world.

'That's my dog,' Philippe told this jumpy-looking young man. 'But you seem to have adopted him.'

'He adopted me.'

'You should be flattered. He's particular – doesn't take to everybody.'

'What's in that bag?'

'Medical equipment. I'm a doctor.'

Philippe opened the bag and let the man see its contents, then closed it.

'So you speak French. That's good, helpful. I think you were in the aircraft that crashed near here. Welcome to France, Monsieur.'

The airman made no reply. He was very pale. Dishevelled and tired, even exhausted. He seemed unsteady on his feet, which gave Philippe concern over his suitability to be in charge of a firearm, particularly when it was pointing at him and held by a hand with a definite tremor. One reason for the man's unsteadiness was plain enough: the left side of the tunic was draped clumsily over his shoulder and a crude bandage was knotted about his arm at the top of the bicep; the bandage had once been white but was now pink, as if it had been bloody but had been rinsed.

'That arm, Monsieur – it would be a good idea to let me take a look at it. And perhaps check you generally.'

'You're a doctor?'

'As I said.'

'How do I know you're not lying?'

Philippe shrugged. 'How do I know you're not a German spy trying to flush out enemies of the Reich?'

'Is that what you are, an enemy of the Reich?'

Philippe waited. The Englishman looked him up and down, seeming to think things over. Then he lowered the pistol, though to Philippe's discomfiture he

107

continued holding it by his side, and nodded for Philippe to approach.

Content that matters were progressing satisfactorily, Eiffel wandered off and stretched himself out at leisure on the forest floor. He yawned.

Philippe, less confident than Eiffel, kept an eye on the pistol while he set the medical bag down. He took out his stethoscope.

'Perhaps you could put the gun away now, Monsieur.'

'Perhaps not.'

Philippe sighed. He began with a few routine checks. The man's breathing was even. But when Philippe tried to take hold of the man's left wrist he winced and stepped back. The pistol rose menacingly.

'Please, Monsieur. Your pulse.'

The airman reluctantly surrendered his arm, which was clearly painful. The pulse, however, was strong and regular. His lungs sounded clear.

There was a damp patch on the ground. Philippe nodded towards it.

'Did you throw up?'

'Yes.'

'Close your eyes, please.'

'No.'

'I want to see how well you can keep your balance.'

'There's nothing wrong with my balance.'

'You're not making things easy, Monsieur. I want you to hold your hands out like this. You can't do it with that gun. Please put it away or set it down.'

In response the man held out his left hand for a moment, though only with difficulty. Then he transferred the gun to that hand – a delicate operation that worried Philippe again – and held out his right. It was an imperfect test, but it was enough for Philippe to see the tremor in both hands.

'Is your vision blurred?'

'It comes and goes. It's good enough to see if you try anything.'

'Watch my finger.' Philippe held up his index finger and moved it from side to side, then towards the airman's nose and away. The man's gaze tracked it accurately.

'Have you experienced any mental confusion?'

'Don't be ridiculous.'

Philippe regarded him in silence for a moment. Then he glanced at the man's forehead.

'You have a head injury.'

'I have two.' The airman turned his head to show the injury on the crown.

Philippe took a small flashlight from his bag and checked each ear. There was no blood. Then he checked each eye. Both pupils were perfectly round and of equal size. They dilated and constricted normally. The head wounds could have been cleaner but at this stage showed no evidence of infection, though that was still a possibility; however, they did not look serious enough to have caused fractures.

'Mild concussion,' pronounced Philippe. He switched off the flashlight. 'You did well to survive the crash.'

'You keep calling it that. It wasn't a crash. It was a good landing under difficult conditions.'

'Well, there was an explosion. Our German friends

have been looking for you.'

'That's not your problem.'

'It is now. They're not very friendly people.'

'No one forced you to come here.'

Philippe nodded in Eiffel's direction. 'He did. Now let's have a look at the arm. Please sit down.'

The Englishman sat down by the stream. Philippe eased the left side of the tunic off, cut the shirtsleeve at the shoulder seam and removed it, careful not to knock against the wound. The bandage turned out to be a long silk scarf. The wound was bad, a sizeable jagged hole, and it had torn the muscle. Philippe rinsed his hands in the stream and probed the surrounding area gently. The airman grimaced but remained silent. Something was certainly embedded in the arm, presumably a bullet. It would be wise to get it out soon. There had probably been considerable loss of blood, which would account for the man's pallor. But he was lucky – so far there was no indication that this wound was infected either.

'Is this yours?' said Philippe. He picked up a knife that was on the ground nearby. It was an outlandish thing with a useless blunt end. 'I trust you weren't thinking of using it on your arm.'

'Certainly not.'

Philippe knew a lie when he heard it. All doctors did. And this was the man's third lie. The first was his claim of experiencing no difficulties with his balance; the second was his denial of mental confusion.

'You're strong and fit,' Philippe told him. 'You'll be fine. You just need to get rid of whatever's in that arm wound.'

'And how will I do that?'

'You won't. I will. But not here. Move closer to the stream, please.'

Philippe scooped handfuls of water from the stream and began to wash the arm wound. The water was the only disinfectant he had; as with so much else, the Germans had a chokehold on medical essentials.

'I've washed it already,' the man pointed out.

Philippe looked at the debris that the water was shifting. 'Stick to flying, Monsieur.'

When the task was done Philippe had another rummage in the medical bag. He had some novocaine, a precious rarity that he had husbanded with care – including not allowing Josette to know about it – and he injected a few milligrams to reduce the pain. Finally he dressed the wound in a clean bandage to protect it from infection.

'Now your head,' he said. 'Lean over the stream.'

'No.'

'There's dirt in the wounds. They could become infected.'

'I'll take that risk.'

'I won't drown you, Monsieur.'

'My head is all right. You've done enough now.'

Philippe sighed and shut the bag. Having done all he could under the circumstances and seeing that his patient was in no immediate danger other than whatever might result from his own pig-headedness – a condition for which no cure had yet been found – Philippe went over to Eiffel, crouched down and scratched the dog's ears.

'Good boy,' he said. Then he bent closer and

whispered so that the Englishman would not hear Albert's name.

'Now go and bring Albert. Find Albert, yes? Go!'

The two men watched as the dog bounded away.

# 18

Philippe learnt that the airman's name was Charlie – which he suspected actually was his real name – but nothing else about him. Which was fine by Philippe. The less he knew, the less would be in jeopardy if things went wrong. That had always been his rule; it had served him and Albert well.

But it was a rule that cut both ways.

'For my part, it's best if you don't know my name,' he told Charlie.

'Whatever you like.'

'Someone will join us shortly. Best for you not to know his identity either.'

Suspicion flashed in the airman's eyes; he picked up the pistol. 'What kind of someone?'

'A good friend. A comrade. You can trust him.'

'You sent the dog for him. Clever dog. Is his name a state secret too?'

'I'd feel better without that gun.'

'I feel better with it. You can always leave if it troubles you that much.'

'You're my patient. I don't abandon my patients, not even when they're as stubborn as mules. I said I'd fix that arm, and I intend to do that. And the gashes on your head.'

'So you'll patch me up. I'm grateful. Then what?'

Philippe shrugged. 'That's up to you. You can leave

my care any time you wish – although I advise you not to be hasty. Until then we'll keep you as safe as we can. We certainly don't plan to hand you over to the authorities or the Germans, if that's what worries you.'

'What worries me is how I get back to England. I've heard it's possible if people help.'

'What people would those be?'

'I'm a fugitive. The Germans are after me. You came here knowing what you'd be letting yourself in for. If you're prepared to do that, then maybe you know others, maybe you have contacts –'

'Let's concentrate on one thing at a time.'

'So you don't deny that it can be done?'

'How would I know?'

For Philippe the conversation had gone far enough. He clamped his lips together and began packing his equipment back into the medical bag.

Then this man called Charlie made a peculiar remark, one that stopped him short.

'You're putting yourself in danger for me, you and your comrade. Like someone else today. An Englishman.'

'In England.'

'No. Here.'

Philippe set the bag down. 'Here? An Englishman? Are you sure?'

'Yes, of course.'

'I don't think so.'

'Why not?'

'I don't know of such a man.'

'You must do. There can't be that many Englishmen around here.'

114

'You're the only one I'm aware of.'

'That can't be.'

'Charlie, I think I'd know if we had another Englishman in this area. Tell me, what does he look like? Maybe you're mistaken in thinking he's English.'

'Well …' Charlie began, then dried up, apparently unable to provide any description. 'I'm not mistaken,' he insisted. 'He's as English as I am.'

Sure enough, concluded Philippe: mental confusion. Or delusion.

'Charlie –' he began, wondering how to put such a delicate suggestion to someone holding a gun. But he broke off when he saw Charlie's face.

The airman was staring right at him but it was clear that he was no longer seeing him. Whatever he was seeing instead – or whatever he was thinking about – had made his already pale complexion as white as a sheet. He moved not a muscle, not even an eyelid. So immobile was he that Philippe's gaze went straight to his throat, to check that a pulse was still beating.

'Charlie?'

Then it was over, as suddenly as it had begun. The airman sucked in a huge breath. He blinked, as if to clear his thoughts, and looked at Philippe – but this time really looked at him.

'Are you all right, Charlie?'

'Of course – why wouldn't I be? I was just thinking about something.'

'The Englishman?'

'What? Don't concern yourself with him. Ignore all that. Ignore what I said.'

'Do you want to tell me what you were thinking?'

'With a question like that, you remind me of someone.'

'Who?'

'Another doctor I met once. In London.'

'What kind of doctor?'

'An unhelpful one.'

'Charlie –'

But that was the moment when Albert chose to arrive, sweaty and gasping for breath after chasing Eiffel.

'My God,' said Albert, staring at the airman and the gun. 'It's true and here he is. Heh, don't shoot,' he added hastily. 'I'm a friend.'

Charlie raised the pistol a little higher. 'I've known this friend for longer.'

'We should be on our way,' said Philippe quickly. 'Charlie, it's a long walk and the forest is difficult terrain. We'll give you a hand.'

'I got here without your help. I don't need it now.'

So they made their way out of the forest. Initially they spaced themselves at intervals of thirty or forty metres, Albert leading and Charlie in the middle, but gradually the airman grew weaker, needing to rest with increasing frequency. It was as Philippe had expected: a cocktail of effects was making itself felt – blood loss, general trauma, exhaustion, delayed impact of the concussion. When Charlie stumbled and almost passed out, he finally gave in and allowed the two brothers to take turns helping him. At last he put the pistol away. By then they had collected Philippe's bicycle, so with one of them half carrying Charlie, the other pushing the bicycle and Eiffel dashing back and forth, they limped back to the farm.

When they were within a field or two, they swung away from the farmhouse and used a route that kept them out of sight of Josette and Pépé, who would still be busy clearing up the wreckage that the Germans had made of their home, and took Charlie directly to the smaller of the farm's two barns, which the brothers always favoured because it was the furthest building from the farmhouse.

Fernand was waiting there already, having figured out that whatever was happening following his father's departure with Eiffel, the barn was where it would end up. The boy was prowling about restlessly but hurried over when the tall door creaked open and Eiffel raced in, followed by the three men.

'Come here,' Albert told his wide-eyed son. 'Outside. Now.'

Philippe steered Charlie into the barn while Albert explained to Fernand that he was not to use anyone's name within the airman's hearing: his uncle, other family members, friends, neighbours.

'He doesn't even know that Philippe and I are brothers. Understand?'

Fernand nodded, unable to take his eyes off the figure in the barn.

'He's not the friendly type,' added Philippe, who came out in time to overhear his brother's words. 'Keep your distance, Fernand. You too, Albert. Let me handle him.'

'Is there a problem?'

'He has a few demons, that's all.'

117

'Demons, heh? Well, we all have those.'

Philippe pressed a bunch of keys into his nephew's hand.

'Go to my house, Fernand. I need you to fetch certain things. Take my bicycle and be as quick as you can.'

He specified the items he needed and detailed where they were to be found, explained which of the keys were for the house, which for the surgery inside the house, and which were for the various secure cabinets and cupboards that Fernand would have to go to in the surgery.

The boy repeated everything back to him until Philippe was satisfied that he had it all correct, then departed.

'Time to prepare our patient,' Philippe told Albert.

Bernard progressed slowly along the lanes that led from his cottage to the village. He was out of breath and the afternoon was still hot; every few paces he stopped to dab his face with a handkerchief stained with engine oil. At these moments he put a hand to his heart to calm it.

It was during one of these recuperative interludes, just as he reached the centre of the village, that he spotted young Fernand Destry, son of Albert and shrewish Josette, and nephew of Philippe the doctor – the very man who was on Bernard's mind at that precise moment, along with a certain German officer and his unreasonable demands and his threats about Bernard's son, threats that would chill any father to the bone.

The village square was a hive of activity and noise – not with villagers going about their innocent daily affairs but with German troopers and their vehicles. Door-to-door searches were in hand of the houses and shops that bordered the square. Trucks and armoured personnel carriers spewed exhaust fumes into the air while armed troopers clomped in and out of the buildings. From every direction came the harsh sound of impatient German voices. Little knots of villagers and shopkeepers watched in forlorn silence as their homes and premises were ransacked and torn apart.

Such searches were something the Germans did regularly as a matter of course, sometimes in Auny's outlying smallholdings and farms, sometimes here in the village itself; but today's search, Bernard realised, would have the special goal of finding the enemy pilot.

Young Fernand Destry was cycling his way around the chaos in the square, taking care not to get in the way of any of the troopers, which was a normal precaution that anyone would take in order not to incur German wrath and the unwanted attention that would follow.

But what piqued Bernard's curiosity was the fact that the lad was riding the doctor's bicycle – in Auny everyone knew everyone else's bicycle – and had come to a halt outside the doctor's house.

Even more intriguing, as Bernard watched, he inserted a key into the door of that house.

Bernard stepped quickly into the alley beside the épicerie, which was closed in the absence of anything to sell.

Now what would Fernand Destry be doing admitting

himself to the doctor's house? Clearly the doctor was not there; if he was, the boy would have no need of a key, he would simply knock.

Bernard scratched a stubbly jowl. The boy could be here for some perfectly innocuous reason. The doctor had forgotten something and Fernand was fetching it for him.

But why could Philippe not fetch it himself?

Well, he was busy, perhaps with a patient.

But what doctor would send an ignorant boy to collect something to do with medical matters, which were not only complex but confidential?

Then perhaps the boy was delivering something, perhaps returning some item to the house on the doctor's behalf.

But he had brought nothing with him.

Bernard chewed things over. He recalled Philippe saying that he was about to make a social call on his brother. Then the aircraft had crashed – a Spitfire, as Bernard had known right from that first moment and declared to Philippe. Following which the doctor had cycled away as if he had just donned the yellow jersey in the Tour de France.

And then the German officer had come calling on Bernard, confirming everything he had thought about the aircraft.

At this, something seemed to constrict Bernard's throat. His heart hammered so hard that he was frightened it would burst and Philippe Destry would be proved right about his parlous health.

Everything was fitting together. A crashed Spitfire; and now that Bernard thought again about that long, graceful glide he and Philippe had watched, the aircraft had seemed to be heading towards Destry land.

Next, a pilot who had survived and was now presumably on the run. Was it beyond the realms of possibility that this pilot might be injured and require medical attention? Was it beyond those same realms of possibility that the Destry brothers would have a hand in whatever that might lead to?

The door of the doctor's house opened. Fernand Destry stuck his nose and head out and looked furtively up and down the street, evidently assessing what the troopers were up to.

Bernard retreated deeper into the alley, sucking his belly in. He peered round the corner.

No troopers were coming young Fernand's way. The lad stepped into the street, locked the door, quickly strapped a small suitcase to the pannier of the bicycle and cycled off in a blur of youthful legs.

Bernard released the breath he was holding and clutched at the wall for support. This was all too much for him, these thoughts that were galloping through his head, the conclusions that leapt into his mind, all this excitement and urgency racing through his veins. It would kill him.

But it might save his son's life if he could find the German officer in time.

# 19

In the corner of the barn there was a charcoal-burning stove, which Albert now hefted outside and lit, using a splash of paraffin to get it going. While the charcoal heated he returned inside and pushed two backless benches together near the door, where the light could fall on them, and over a drain gully that divided the floor of the barn. He fetched water from the pump outside and began to scrub the benches down.

Eiffel watched him for a while, then ambled over to Philippe, who was advising Charlie.

'Take all your clothes off,' he instructed. 'Not just the uniform, everything. Everything must be destroyed, burnt, even civilian items. This scarf you were using as a bandage – where would an ordinary person around here get a silk scarf? You need to become a Frenchman, wearing French clothes.

'But there's something you must consider. Once your clothes and uniform have gone and you put on other clothing, if the Germans capture you, you'll be classified as a spy because you're in disguise. You'll forfeit your right to be treated as a prisoner of war. After interrogation – which won't be pleasant, I promise you – you'll be executed. So think carefully, Charlie. If you don't want to go ahead, I'll still treat your injuries and then you can turn yourself in.'

'Why would I do that when you're going to get me

back to England?'

'Charlie, I've never said –'

'No need. I've been watching you two. You're no strangers to this, you've done it before.'

As Charlie spoke, he took something from his pocket. A photograph; Philippe could not see of whom or what, but he could guess. Its edges were worn and no longer crisp, the corners split and crushed from the many times it had been handled and gazed at. The airman set it on a nearby packing case, face down, glancing at Philippe as he did so, almost as if the act of parting with it was a token of trust. Then he placed the pistol and his knife beside it, followed by a spare magazine of bullets and a few banknotes, all francs.

Philippe understood what was happening. This was a long way from the jumpy young man who would not even close his eyes at his request. Nor was this the man with the catatonic stare that had alarmed him. This was a man who was calm and lucid and recognised that their lives were now completely in each other's hands.

Albert collected the airman's clothing, put each garment into the stove and poked it down over the charcoal until it was consumed. Every now and then he scraped the ash into a tin bucket and splashed more paraffin on the charcoal.

Philippe explained to Charlie that the uniform's metal buttons would be extracted from the ash and dumped in a nearby lake along with the boots, which would be weighted with rocks.

'Like I said,' replied the airman. 'You're no novices.'

123

Philippe told him to lie down on the benches. Albert arrived with a bucket filled to the brim with water. A hole at the base was plugged by a wine cork.

'I'm going to irrigate your arm wound again,' Philippe told Charlie. 'But more thoroughly than was possible in the forest. Also the injuries to your head. And without arguments this time, please. Are you ready?'

The airman nodded.

Albert hoisted the heavy bucket above him, removed the cork and for the next ten minutes allowed water to pour over the wounds as Philippe directed, while the doctor scrutinised them and occasionally dabbed away particles of dirt and loose scraps of flesh with a piece of clean gauze or plucked them out with tweezers.

The water was cold. At the end of the procedure Charlie was shaking like a leaf. But he had uttered not a word of protest nor a single moan of pain. Philippe wrapped a temporary bandage about the arm to keep it clean and dressed the head wounds. Then he covered his patient with a clean blanket that Albert had fetched from a chest hidden behind an ancient pony trap, and looked up just as Fernand hurtled into the barn and leapt off the bicycle.

'You have everything?' Philippe asked him.

Fernand nodded.

Philippe exhaled. Now came the real work.


As the search of the houses in the village square progressed, the German officer became aware that the garage owner was watching him. But he was used to being watched by these people and at first thought nothing of it. And besides, the man was probably still stinging from their encounter earlier.

What was his name? Bernard something. It was on the list. A drunk. Had a son in the Ruhr mines.

But this Bernard was not simply watching him; he was staring fixedly at him. Which was a different thing and a sure and certain route to being clapped in a cell.

So the officer met Bernard's gaze and held it.

The garage owner did not look away, which these people usually did. An odd sequence of expressions flitted over his face. His head twitched to one side. The officer realised that he was trying to wink and signal that he wanted to speak to him. Not here but somewhere discreet.

So the officer climbed aboard the little bucket jeep and extricated it from the trucks and other vehicles. He bumped over the pavement and turned down the narrow street behind Bernard. He pulled in and waited.

It took the garage owner ten minutes to reach him, his feet slapping on the pavement, his arms dangling in that strange way of walking he had. He was puffing like a wheezy train by the time he arrived.

But the officer listened carefully to what he had to say between puffs.

Philippe had an uneasy feeling that there might not be enough novocaine.

'I can dull the pain a little, Charlie,' he explained as he injected the last of the painkiller. 'But that's all. I can't eliminate it. And I don't know how long the effect will last.'

The airman was still shivering but nodded that he

125

understood.

Albert scrubbed down a plank and placed it across some bricks to form a low table at the foot of the benches on which Charlie was lying and at right angles to them. He unrolled a clean linen cloth, one of the items that Fernand had fetched, spread it along the plank and set out the other items – surgical instruments, gauze, bandages, needles, a small jar containing sterile catgut sutures.

With the burning of the airman's clothing complete, Albert and Fernand carried the stove into the barn, lifting it on two spars of timber since it was too hot to touch. They positioned it at the head of the benches and to Philippe's right. This would allow his instruments to be placed directly in his hand after being sterilised.

Fernand was despatched to the inner recesses of the barn with orders to remain there in stillness and silence. He took with him the small suitcase. All it held now was a change of clothing for Charlie.

Philippe and Albert went out to the pump and scrubbed their hands and arms with soap. They had no surgical garments, no masks, no gloves, and in the barn there was no lighting other than the rays of the afternoon sun streaming through the open door.

Philippe took a deep breath and surveyed his makeshift operating theatre. It was the best he could do.

The novocaine should have taken effect by now. He pressed the flesh around the arm wound.

'Can you feel this, Charlie? Or this? This?'

The airman shook his head each time.

Philippe had wrapped the handle of a scalpel in gauze so that Albert could hold the blade in the stove until the metal turned red. It was now cool enough to be used. But the airman's entire body stiffened as soon as the blade began to cut. Philippe's heart sank. It was as he had feared: the novocaine was inadequate.

'Charlie, I need you to be very still. Try to relax.'

The airman uttered a dry laugh. There were beads of sweat on his brow and haggard face. But his eyes closed, as if he was absenting himself from the situation, like an Eastern mystic. The arm slowly relaxed and the tautness left the muscles.

Philippe continued the incision, cutting where the bullet was lodged. As the blood welled he mopped it himself; he had no nurse and Albert was busy sterilising the forceps for the next stage of the procedure. This was surgery in the raw, from first principles, surgery as it had been a century ago.

When the forceps had cooled, Philippe slipped them gently into the incision and contrary to his expectation gripped the bullet on his first attempt. It came out smoothly. There was a metallic clink as he dropped it into the small steel kidney dish that Albert was holding.

Both men peered down at the dish. But instead of the rounded contours of a bullet they saw an irregularly shaped fragment of metal. Its irregularity of form was what had made it easy to grip.

'Shrapnel, I think,' Philippe told Charlie without looking up. 'We'll see properly when it's been washed.'

Thinking that his work was done, he pressed his

fingers gently on the flesh around the wound. It was a precautionary step, no more than that, before closing the incision and suturing it.

But something was still in there.

He inserted the forceps again, went straight to where the unexpected lump was.

Another easy find. Another clink of metal on metal as he deposited it in the kidney dish.

Again the two brothers peered into the dish, their heads almost touching. Then Albert poured a little water into the dish and tipped it to drain. There was now no question what the object was.

'Heh,' said Albert as he washed and dabbed both objects dry and wrapped them in a fold of gauze.

'Charlie …' said Philippe.

No reply.

Philippe straightened up and looked more closely at his patient.

'Charlie?'

The English airman was no longer on a higher plane of consciousness. He had passed out.

'No bad thing,' said Philippe. 'Gives his body time to recover.'

He slipped the fold of gauze and its contents into his pocket for safekeeping. Then with Albert's help he washed out the incision and stitched it closed.

Just as he was finishing, Eiffel, who had been dozing nearby, rose abruptly to his feet and retreated deeper into the barn, whimpering.

Philippe looked up to see what was troubling the little dog. A movement behind him caught his eye. He turned round.

Josette was standing in the doorway. She was leaning on one of Pépé's walking sticks and wearing one of her husband's boots, the only footwear large enough to accommodate her bandaged foot.

She was staring at the unconscious man, her eyes like saucers, her mouth wide open.

# 20

At Philippe's insistence they vacated the barn. What his patient certainly did not need was Josette's harangues blazing around him.

And they were fearsome, those harangues. They exploded into life even before Philippe closed the barn door, they continued across the barnyard and past the cowshed and the milking parlour, they found new impetus as Josette hounded her men past the woodshed, the large barn and the henhouses, they blasted about their ears and roared unabated into the farmhouse with them. They were scolds that would have stunned birds on the wing and brought them tumbling from the sky. Josette shrieked at all three Destry males in turn, lunged at Albert with the walking stick – her injured foot no impediment – boxed her son's ears, damned Philippe to hell, accusing him and his worthless brother of luring her innocent child into their web of folly and danger.

In the farmhouse Eiffel shrank into a corner, his tail down and his left ear flattened against his head. He placed a paw protectively over the bent right ear.

But Pépé, when he gathered what all the fuss was about, was over the moon. He slapped his sons on the back, shook their hands, grinned at them through his broken teeth, hugged his grandson and burst into a tuneless Marseillaise.

'You're men, not worms after all,' he crowed. 'You too, my lad,' he told Fernand. 'Thank God I lived to see this day.'

Josette cuffed the old man. He responded with a stream of obscenities.

There was no telling how long the fireworks could have continued had they not been interrupted by the roar of vehicles and the screech of tyres in the farmyard. German vehicles, German tyres. Closely followed by the shouting of German voices.

Philippe went to the window and there they were: three truckloads of troopers again, bristling with rifles, plus the same officer as before in his dusty Kübelwagen.

The officer placed the household under armed guard, just as he had done the last time, while he and half a dozen of the troopers banged their way through the house, which had not yet been properly set to rights since their previous visit. The rest of the detachment fanned out across the farm.

'Merde,' said Albert.

'You don't let me say that,' Fernand reminded him.

'Merde.'

'I'll kill you, Albert Destry.'

'Won't have to, Josette. They'll do it for you. Cheer up, we'll die together. That's a good thing, heh?'

Josette sobbed.

'Never understood why you married her,' Pépé told his son.

'Schweigen Sie!' snarled a trooper.

Pépé swore at him, then lapsed into silence.

Eiffel chose a moment when no hulking bodies with

their big boots were blocking the doorway and made his escape.

'Good boy,' said Philippe under his breath. He wondered how the dog would get by without him.

Something was happening. A trooper came running at full tilt across the yard and clattered upstairs to where the officer was supervising the search of the bedrooms. Philippe heard a burst of excited German from the trooper followed by a series of sharply delivered questions from the officer. The trooper's confidence increased with each reply he made.

'Merde,' said Albert again. 'It's over.'

Philippe looked across at Fernand. The last time the farm had been searched, he had reassured the boy that they would not be shot. There could be no such reassurances this time. The lad smiled sorrowfully at him, thinking the same thing.

The officer came downstairs. He issued an order to the troopers, who prodded the family out of the house at gunpoint. To be put against the wall and shot, was Philippe's guess.

But not just yet, apparently. The officer retraced in reverse the journey they themselves had made not long previously under Josette's tongue-lashing. They followed him, guns at their backs. Josette, hobbling along with the aid of the walking stick, had ceased sobbing, as if resigned to her fate. Even Pépé held his tongue.

Across the farmyard they went, past the henhouses, the large barn and the woodshed, the milking parlour and the cowshed, until they arrived at the small barn. Philippe steeled himself. So this was where it would be. This was where he would die. Where all of them would die.

The barn was surrounded by troopers now, rifles posed casually across their chests. One man sprang to the door and flung it open as the officer approached.

The officer pushed Albert through the doorway. The troopers prodded the others inside after him.

Philippe looked around. Yes, here were the two benches pushed together, the blanket now cast aside on the floor. Here was the stove, its charcoal still burning. Here was the bucket. Here were his surgical instruments and the kidney dish. Here were the hanks of blood-soaked gauze and the drain gulley with half-flushed streaks of blood. Everything was just as he and Albert had left it.

Apart from Charlie.

Charlie was gone.


'Hurry up, Charlie,' the stranger had insisted.

To Charlie it had been as if the day was repeating itself, caught in a loop. He had regained consciousness to the sound of the man's voice urging him to wake up, just as had happened before, and then he seemed to be struggling to the surface of spiralling currents in which he saw Émilie and little Charlie again, then the skies of France spinning past him and the earth rushing up to him as the Spitfire dived, then this stranger standing beside him as he tried to gather his wits together. All just as before.

Except the stranger really was here, although not standing by the Spitfire, and this time Charlie was stretched out stark naked on cold, damp wood. There were strips of bandage on his head, and his left arm felt as if someone had tried to saw it off – in fact, was still trying.

Again it was a question of which version of reality to believe, which one to live out. In this version, gradually he remembered things since his time in the forest, as if they were parts of the day's patchwork that would eventually assemble into a whole. He saw that he was in the barn. He was able to remember how he had got here. He remembered the two men, one of them the doctor with clean pale hands, the other a rougher type with weathered hands to match, perhaps a farmer. There was also a boy, but the doctor had sent him away. Fragmented memories of his medical treatment came back to him; he wondered if the shrapnel had been removed from his arm. Certainly he remembered a blade piercing the flesh and the fearsome pain that caused. After which, nothing, a blank.

He was freezing cold. His hands had been shaking earlier; now his whole body was doing so. And somehow he knew he had to get away from here, from this barn, from the farm. At once. Danger was imminent, rushing towards him like the earth of France had done. Had the stranger told him about the danger? Perhaps. Hard to be sure. Hard to be sure of anything at all.

The stranger. Charlie continued to think of him as that. He remembered quizzing the doctor about him. He remembered the doctor's denial of knowing any such person.

So hard to be sure of anything. Even what the

stranger looked like, that forgettable man. But there was the realisation that had surged through Charlie at that moment of the doctor's denial, like the burst of St Elmo's fire that had danced on his aircraft once when he was caught in a thunderstorm – a cold blue flame of certainty.

Could he be right?

So hard to be sure of anything. Especially the impossible.

But he *was* right.

He found some clothes in a small suitcase and dressed as quickly as his arm and shivering body would allow. He guessed the clothes were intended for him because he remembered his own being destroyed. These replacements were work clothes, exactly what the doctor with the calm hands had said he was lacking: a blue cotton shirt, the bleu de travail that every French working man wore in city or countryside; shabby trousers; a pair of ancient and thoroughly scuffed work boots; and an old flat cap, also in faded blue cotton, that would hide the dressings on his head.

He found his possessions where he had left them on the packing case. He put everything safely away in his pockets and slipped the Browning into his waistband, concealed by the loose shirt.

There was a patch of weedy ground behind the barn overgrown by clumps of comfrey and sprinkled with sprays of stitchwort, and after that a fence woven from strips of hazel. He recalled the stands of coppiced hazel in the forest, as if every detail like that was part of the loop. This fence was tumbling down; it was easy to step across to the narrow lane on the other side.

The stranger was waiting there for him. Naturally.

'No time to lose,' he said. 'It's you they're coming for.'

Charlie heard the heavy rumble of truck engines not far away. Tyres thumped over potholes. He heard the clank and rattle of metal and wood as the frames of the vehicles shook. They would be German vehicles and they were moving at speed. He had to do the same, move at speed. The stranger was right.

But he always was. Charlie remembered that too.

So where was he to go now? He had to be able to find his way back to the doctor and the farmer when it became safe for him to do so – assuming that such a time would come and that they would still be at liberty if it did. All his instincts had said they were his best chance of getting back to England and he still stuck by that.

He took his bearings from the late afternoon sun. Beyond the lane to the west stretched open fields and presumably more farms. Friendly or not? No way of knowing. To the south and east, more fields, with the same unanswerable question. North of him was where the vehicles were arriving – which had to be the entrance of the farm to which the barn belonged. In that direction was the route along which the doctor and the farmer had brought him earlier; he had caught glimpses of farm buildings as they skirted them.

It came down to instincts again. After searching the farm itself, the Germans would most likely go on to search the land beyond it. They were less likely to search in the direction from which they had just come.

136

Better therefore to go north. Doing that, he might stand a chance.

'Go north,' said the stranger. 'You might stand a chance.'

Stranger? Hardly a stranger after all.

'What about you?' said Charlie.

'It's safer for you to travel alone.'

Charlie was watching the fields. Nothing was stirring, no worker was to be seen, there was no glint of sunlight reflecting from a German helmet or gun.

A sudden movement took his attention. A hare broke cover, a hawk fell upon it and bore it away. The hare's squeals echoed over the fields.

He was wrong. Death was stirring.

When he turned round to reply to the man – this stranger who was no stranger at all – to speak the words he had formed, he found himself alone. Another of the stranger's vanishing tricks.

'I know who you are,' he told the empty air anyway.

# 21

'Where is he?' demanded the German officer.

Philippe said nothing. Fernand said nothing. Josette said nothing. Pépé deposited a mouthful of phlegm on the barn floor and said nothing.

'Who?' said Albert.

The officer closed in on him. 'The English pilot.'

'No idea what you're talking about.'

'Don't play the fool. This is your farm. Where are you hiding him?'

'It's my farm, in fact,' Pépé corrected him.

'Be quiet, Pépé,' said Albert.

'Shut me up if you want but the farm's still mine.'

The officer produced the Luger and barked something in German, then swung round to confront Philippe. He shoved the Luger into his gut.

'You're the doctor. You operated on him here. The evidence is all around you.'

His words provoked a mighty hoot of laughter from Josette. They all jumped, startled, including the German. Albert looked terrified, understandably wondering what the German's reaction would be.

Anxious that the Luger could go off accidentally, Philippe sidled out of its line of fire. The officer failed to notice, his attention now on the bizarre madwoman wearing a single unlaced boot, a man's at that, and leaning on a walking stick.

'It was me!' she screeched at him. Her eyes swivelled and flecks of spit flew from her lips. 'It was me he operated on! Me, you fool!'

She jabbed her chest. Philippe watched in awe. All four Destry males did. Her bosom rippled like the cream in her butter churn that would never see another working day.

'He had to, because you and your buffoons almost cut my foot off! I could have died!'

It was obvious that the German was unable to understand everything that spilled from her mouth but the drift was clear enough, especially when she tore off the boot, unravelled the bandage it was concealing and seized Albert's shoulder so that she could stick her naked foot in the air for the officer to see.

The cut was deep. It ran the width of her foot. Philippe sighed to see his handiwork undone. He had sutured the wound with care but Josette's marches to and from the barn, the attacks she had launched on Albert and Fernand and now her violent removal of the bandage, all this had torn the stitches. A chunk of flesh on the sole of her foot flapped open, its interior lined like tree rings. Fresh blood dripped to the barn floor.

The German blanched, which Philippe found interesting. Was this a warmonger who quailed at the sight of blood?

'May we go now?' enquired Albert. 'Will you leave us alone at last? And will you get your men and vehicles off my land?'

'My land,' said Pépé.

Charlie stayed as far away from the lane as he could,

guessing that it was the only way into and out of the farm. It would be the route the Germans would take when they departed. So he stuck to the furthest boundaries of the fields that ran alongside it, using ditches and hedges for cover when they ran in the direction he needed, but always keeping an eye on the lane.

He met no one and never laid eyes on another human being. This emptiness of the country was eerie but not unexpected. The stories reaching England said that almost a hundred thousand men had perished in the few weeks it had taken for France to fall last year and perhaps one and a half million were being held by Germany as prisoners of war. The great majority were men who had worked the land; and now the land was without them. As in England, it fell to women to take over alongside those who remained, such as the farmer he had encountered today. But there were not enough women. The result was the deserted landscape.

So Charlie plodded on, the beneficiary of this emptiness. An ill wind, he said to himself.

After a mile or so he spotted rooftops and a church spire and recalled that he had passed over a small hamlet as he was bringing the crippled Spitfire down. He veered away.

He saw the hayfield when he was still about half a mile off. He felt like a traveller happening upon a mirage in the desert. But the hayfield and its wonderful aroma were real. He found half-built haystacks, two pitchforks abandoned beside them as if those who had been using them – whether men or women – had just this moment quit their labour. And might return to it just as suddenly, which was a concern.

But it was a risk worth taking. Anyway, the truth was he had no choice, could go no further. He was worn out, his arm and head were screaming blue murder, he felt as if one more step was the step that would finish him off.

He let his grateful body collapse on the hay.

Pépé, Albert and Fernand stayed in the barn while Philippe tended to Josette's foot again and Josette said her piece. Fernand and Pépé stood at a safe distance. Philippe kept his head down, in more ways than one, concentrating on sutures and bandages. These he had trained for; he had never trained for Josette.

'How stupid do you think I am, Albert Destry?' she began. 'I've always known, of course I have. I'm a woman. You men think we're as stupid as you. Big mistake. You're the stupid ones. I wake in the middle of the night and you're not in our bed. Not in the house either. I come outside to look for you and there are lights here in the barn. Shadows flitting about like ghosts. Then there's you with this one.' She meant Philippe. 'As thick as thieves, whispering in corners, day and night. I go into the village and there you are when you're supposed to be in the fields working, you're talking to someone I've never set eyes on before, so it's someone who doesn't even come from Auny. Food goes missing – am I supposed to think it's mice? Mice with man-sized appetites?

'And as for you, Philippe Destry, I see as much of you these days, God help me, as I do of my husband.

141

You might as well be living with us. It didn't take a genius to know the two of you were up to no good. Even Fernand guessed something was going on. The only thing I didn't know was exactly what it was. But whatever it was, I knew you shouldn't be doing it.'

'You said nothing.'

'What should I have said, Albert? What would have stopped you?'

'I wouldn't call it no good, what we're doing.'

'All the same, it took you long enough,' muttered Pépé.

'Shut up, you old fool,' Josette told her father-in-law. 'Well, good or bad, there's no going back. Not for any of us.'

She examined her freshly bandaged foot and tugged Albert's boot back on without bothering to thank Philippe.

So he thanked her instead.

'You saved us, Josette,' he said meekly. 'And the English airman.'

She turned her hardest gaze on him.

'Keep your thanks, Philippe Destry. I want no thanks from anyone, least of all you. You've never liked me. No – don't argue, it's true. Perhaps after today I can expect better from you in future than I've had so far in my years with your brother, but always remember that whatever you think of what I did, I didn't do it for you. I didn't even do it for France. I did it for these two.' She tossed her head towards Albert and Fernand. Her hair fell across her face. 'And I did it because why should the Germans take everything we've worked for?' She turned to her husband. 'I won't have our

142

only child arrested by those monsters or watch him growing up in a place that's only a province of Germany. You and I, we've lost enough in our lives already, Albert – no, we've lost too much. Those nights when I woke and you weren't there, I thought … Well, you know what I thought. And I had to go looking for you because –'

Her voice broke. Albert reached for her hand but she brushed him away. She drew deep breaths, her eyes closed, her chest heaving. No one dared speak, not even Pépé, less a monarch now than a serf, as all of them were. They waited in silence. Philippe busied himself with packing the medical bag.

'So what happens now?' she demanded of Albert and Philippe when her voice was under control. 'Not even you two can delude yourselves that we're in the clear just because we convinced the Germans this time. If they catch up with the Englishman we're finished. He'll send them straight to us.'

'He won't. He can't. He doesn't know who we are. We didn't give our names.'

'Ha! And he can't describe you, is that what you think? Or this place? If you believe that, Albert, you're even more stupid than I thought. We'd better hope they don't find him.'

Philippe sighed. There was no arguing with that.

Josette was quiet, thinking.

'So you're the ones that have to do it,' she announced.

'Have to do what?' said Albert.

'Find him,' supplied Fernand, unable to hold himself back, his mind, as always, ahead of everyone else's.

143

Except his mother's, of course.

'Exactly that,' confirmed Josette. 'Your son has a brain, Albert, even if you don't. Find the Englishman – and fast, before the Germans do. Bring him back here so that you can do with him whatever you did with the others who passed through here. They're not here now, so obviously you have a way of passing them on. Find the Englishman, that's what you must do. And you'd better be quick about it.'

Philippe and Albert looked at one another. There was no arguing with that either.

The German officer had blanched not at the sight of the Frenchwoman's blood – he would have been pleased to open her veins himself – but at the realisation that he had been humiliated yet again.

There had been the empty Spitfire. Then the first fruitless search of the Destry farm. The abortive hunt in the forest. And then the second search of the Destry place, which for a glorious few moments in the barn seemed about to vindicate all his efforts and assert him as a man who got results.

But as soon as that hag raised her foot he knew he had failed again. And as before, in full view of his troopers. Who would not blanche at such rank and public failure?

He flung the Kübelwagen into the garage yard, screeched to a halt and leapt out. Blood was exactly what he wanted. Not the Frenchwoman's but the garage owner's. It would mean one less informer on his list, but the man had never produced any intelligence worth a Reichspfennig.

He searched the yard, he searched between and around all the decaying remnants of vehicles and farm machinery and engines. The cottage door had been left unlocked; he searched each pathetic little room, all of which stank. He stalked the nearest fields for a while but that too was pointless.

He thought about what to do. He could wait until the garage owner returned from wherever he was. Yes, that was a good idea. He returned to the Kübelwagen and sat there, his feet up on the dash, drumming his fingers and looking all around and thinking about the nice things he was going to do to Bernard when he got his hands on him.

But as time ticked by this waiting seemed to be not such a good idea after all. It was that time in the late afternoon when the August heat was at its most oppressive, more dense than at noon, having baked the land all through the day so that the air was thick and the heat lay like a solid crust. His little vehicle had no roof, it offered no shade and, worst of all, it provided no protection from the stench of that septic tank. He began to feel ill. He became too hot. He began to sweat. He began to wonder what airborne infections he was exposing himself to. Every breath he took might be filling his lungs with unimaginable hordes of parasites and bacteria. His skin began to crawl. He began to sweat more heavily. Was it anxiety or was some disease taking hold already?

Eventually it was more than he could bear. He started the engine, put his foot to the floor and raced back to barracks as fast as the twisting lanes with their high hedges and steep earth banks and blind corners would allow.

He was thankful to have clean air in his lungs, but anxiety for his health still weighed heavily on his thoughts. He should not have lingered at the cottage. He had put himself at risk. The more he thought about this, the faster he drove. The faster he drove, the harder he had to concentrate on those sharp bends, and the less he took in his surroundings.

When he sped past a hay meadow, the scent of the freshly mown hay filled his nostrils and was so intoxicating that he hardly noticed the two men who were standing beside a tall rick, one of them busily forking hay while the other used an old blue cap to wipe sweat from his face, his pitchfork cradled in the crook of his arm.

Nor did the officer give any thought to the small white dog that was scampering at their feet in the deep swathes of cut stalks.

## 22

There were four civilian telephones in Auny-sous-Bois. The mayor had one; which was to say his office had one. The priest had one, in his sacristy. The postmaster had one, in his post office. And Philippe Destry, being a doctor, had one, in his surgery.

He was still breathless from his cycle ride from the farm. He forced himself to wait until his breathing settled down before dialling the number.

It rang only once. In Philippe's experience it only ever rang once. Did someone sit there all day long and all night, waiting for it to ring?

A woman answered, with just one word: 'Yes?'

Even in that single syllable he recognised her. He had spoken to her before. He wondered what she looked like. He always wondered. She sounded young. There were others, male and female. All of them seemed young but he reckoned she was the youngest.

'Maître Crow was perched on a tree,' he said.

His voice was carefully toneless but clear and level. He had to sound the part. In his imagination the day would come when they would finally meet. She would win his heart when so many others had failed.

'Holding a cheese in his beak,' she replied, just as expressionlessly.

'This is Florian. I have a consignment.'

'One?'

'One, yes.'

There was a pause. She would be checking where Florian was located and comparing that with planned movements and their schedules. She knew more about him than he did about her. All he had was this Paris telephone number. Just as silly Bernard had said, the capital was one of the places where things wcrc starting, even if they did not yet take the form the garagiste hoped for – though that might come soon enough.

Philippe waited patiently. The young woman might tell him a week or she might say a month. It depended on factors he could not guess at.

When the answer came, it took him by surprise.

'Tonight,' she said.

Tonight? So soon? Such a possibility had never occurred to him. This had never happened before.

But Josette would be relieved. That was something, he supposed. If they could manage it.

'Are you still there?' she said.

'I apologise. Tonight may be too soon.'

She remained unperturbed. 'You will have ten minutes. Not a minute more.'

Such calm authority in that young voice.

'And if it's not possible?'

'Call again when it is.'

She hung up.

Bernard waited until the whine of the Kübelwagen could no longer be heard, then squeezed himself out from the seatless cabin of the decrepit old Berliet delivery van where he had taken refuge. The cabin was not only seatless but was airless as well, and he was dripping with sweat.

He gulped air and ran the oil-stained handkerchief over his face and neck as he tried to regain a tolerable operating temperature. He had heard the German strutting about his yard, passing within a metre of him numerous times, swearing as he went, heard him slamming the cottage door open and hammering up and down the stairs looking for him, heard him swearing some more as he returned to the Kübelwagen. But instead of driving off he just stayed there. And stayed.

Until finally, mercifully, Bernard heard the engine start and the vehicle drove away.

He had no idea why the German had come calling on him this time, no idea whether it was connected with his pursuit of the English pilot at the Destry farm. Nor did he care. It no longer mattered.

All that mattered was the letter that had been waiting for him when he got home earlier. It was in French but it had come from Germany. It informed him that his son was dead. An accident, although it did not say what kind of accident or where. It commended the fact that his son had died giving valuable service to the Reich.

Bernard knew the truth. His boy had died – in effect had been murdered – a kilometre underneath the alien soil of Germany, tearing German coal from a rock face, his lungs clogged with German dirt.

So the last person in the world Bernard wanted to see was the German officer. Or any other German. In fact, he did not want to see anyone. He wanted to think about his son. He wanted to be left in peace to mourn.

But he was also filled with hatred. And he wanted to think about what he was going to do about that.


'He's gone,' said Fernand as the vehicle disappeared into the distance, a cloud of dust above the hedgerows marking its passage. He tossed his pitchfork aside.

'You're sure that was him?' said the English airman, who had introduced himself as Charlie.

'That was him, Charlie. I'm positive.'

'When the trucks went past, I took it that was the lot. I wonder what delayed him.'

'He's the boss. He can do as he pleases.'

Fernand was on top of the world. First he had found Eiffel – strictly speaking, Eiffel had found him – then they had both found the airman. It was simple. Fernand had wondered where he himself would hide if he was on the run. The answer was somewhere not too far from the farm and within sight of its one lane, which the Germans would have to use; perhaps a good big field so that he could put himself safely distant from the lane; and preferably with somewhere or something in which to hide – such as a haystack.

Not only was he correct on all points, but now here he was, on first-name terms with the airman – well, apart from his own name, of course, as his father had insisted – and the man was perfectly agreeable despite Uncle Philippe's warning. Best of all, they were even working together to dupe the Boche.

'Let's get back to the farm,' said Charlie. 'I think it's safe now.'

He was still carrying his pitchfork, cradled in the

crook of his injured left arm. He picked up Fernand's fork and handed it back to him.

'We're workers, remember? We treat our tools with respect. Right?'

Fernand felt himself blushing.

'Right, Charlie,' he said. 'Absolutely right.'

The two of them set off, Eiffel leading the way.

## 23

'Henry,' said Émilie in surprise when she opened the door and saw him standing there. Her eyes brightened with the beginnings of a smile.

Henry was in uniform now – he had judged it appropriate for what was in principle an official visit – but had removed his cap.

But cap or not, the uniform said it all. Said far too much, in fact.

Émilie's smile fled. She reached down to grasp the hand of the toddler – little Charlie – who had tottered after her to the door.

'Oh no, Henry. Please – no.'

She hurriedly lifted the child in her arms as if to protect him and stepped back, her face taut with fear, but Henry reached forward and laid his thin hand on her arm.

'Missing,' he said quickly. 'That's all, Émilie, my dear. Only missing.' Kingdom's words echoed in his mind. 'You must hold on to that, Émilie. We both must.'

'You'd better come in,' she said.


'The Air Vice-Marshal will see you now, sir.'

Percy Kingdom entered the office and saluted.

The distinguished grey-haired man standing at the large table in the centre of the room returned the salute, but his version was more casual – never one to stand on ceremony, the Air Vice-Marshal. He continued scrutinising the map that covered the entire surface of the table.

'How's your father-in-law, Percy?' he asked without looking up. 'Sit yourself down, man – sit, sit. Be right with you.'

'He's very well, sir. Thoughtful of you to ask.'

'Give him my best. Enjoyed myself with him at Cheltenham back in March.'

'Poet Prince, wasn't it, sir, for the Gold Cup?'

'The very one. Good odds too, as I recall.'

The Air Vice-Marshal left the table and seated himself behind the desk, opposite Kingdom. He lit a cigarette.

'Now, what's on your mind, Percy?'

'Somewhat sensitive situation, sir. Mind if I join you?' Kingdom produced the Dunhill briar. 'One of my pilots – best one, in fact – well, he's put himself in a spot of bother. Unauthorised sortie, went out solo. Consequence, he's gone missing. Nothing much we can do at this moment. Wait and see. The tricky part concerns what happens if he shows up – which, of course, we hope he will.'

The Air Vice-Marshal frowned. 'Not sure I follow. If he shows up, you celebrate. That's what happens. Especially if he's your best. Couldn't be simpler.'

'Of course, sir. But according to the book he's broken a few rules. Could even say he stole an aircraft. Technically speaking, he should be disciplined.'

'I see. And your suggestion is?'

'To do nothing of the sort, sir.'

'Good man. Bugger the book. Technically speaking. There's a war on. If the prodigal comes back, kill the fatted calf.'

Biblical again, thought Kingdom.

'Quite so, sir,' he replied.

# 24

'Wake up,' the voice said. 'Time to wake up, Charlie!'

A man's voice again. Was the day in that damned loop again?

No, there was no loop – because this time the voice was speaking in French.

Charlie woke immediately. No struggling up from the depths, no confused images to blunt his thinking. Wide awake at once, sharp and ready. What would happen now was what he had hoped and waited for.

The flashlight shining in his face moved aside. The rest of the barn beyond its beam was in darkness. It was night, sometime in the small hours, because that was what he had been told to expect, and he was learning that these people stuck to their word.

He made out the features and bald pate of the doctor. That was who had woken him and was holding the flashlight. Other people were moving about behind him, none of them speaking. It was the same air of noiseless efficiency that had characterised the doctor and the farmer when they disposed of his clothing and prepared to operate on him.

The figures came closer and he recognised the farmer and the boy who had tracked him down in the hayfield. A small splash of white meandered across the floor towards him. It was the little dog. Then he saw that these familiar figures had been joined by a woman. She was limping.

This made him think about his arm. He flexed it cautiously as he stood up. Definitely feeling better. His head felt better too, the headache now gone, and his tremble too. These several hours' sleep had helped but most of all he had the doctor and his field surgery skill to thank.

'We must leave soon,' the doctor was saying. 'The people we're to meet will wait for only ten minutes. Not a minute more.'

The woman came closer. A curl of dark hair fell across her face. She pushed it away but it fell forward again. A good-looking woman. She handed Charlie a leather bag with a shoulder strap, like a worker's tool bag.

'Food,' she explained. She seemed embarrassed to be offering a gift. 'Plenty of food in there. You have a long journey ahead, Monsieur Charlie.'

A brief, shy smile, like a child's, then she limped away.

The boy approached. He extended his hand.

'Good luck, Charlie,' he said. He grinned broadly. 'I'll watch the sky. I'll be looking for you.'

They shook hands, then the boy too was gone.

'This is yours,' said the doctor. 'A souvenir. It's what I found in your arm.'

He dropped a small, heavy chunk of metal into Charlie's hand and shone the flashlight on it. It was a piece of shrapnel. Charlie smiled. Not just any old piece of shrapnel. It was a piece of his Spitfire.

'Then there's this.' The doctor followed the shrapnel with a second object, this one much lighter. 'I think perhaps it was in your breast pocket and the shrapnel drove it into your arm. Which means the shrapnel just missed you, Charlie, you had a very narrow escape.'

Charlie looked down. Despite the damage it had taken, he recognised the St Christopher medallion.

'You were lucky, yes?' said the doctor.

'Yes,' said Charlie. He was no longer smiling.

'So it seems you're a religious man.'

'I'm not.'

'Considering everything, perhaps you should be,' suggested the farmer, who was watching and listening. There was gentle reproach in his tone. 'But if you're not, why do you have the St Christopher?'

Charlie rubbed the mangled piece of silver between finger and thumb, feeling its twists and broken sharpnesses. As sharp as memory.

'It belonged to a friend. He always carried it with him. Never flew without it.'

'You speak in the past tense, Charlie.'

No answer. Charlie's thoughts were on that last sortie. And it *was* the last one with Kemp; he knew that now.

'A fellow airman, perhaps?' prompted the farmer.

'He was running to his aircraft. The medallion fell from his pocket. He didn't notice. I picked it up, to give it back to him. I called but he didn't hear. Lot of noise going on – Spitfires taking off, every aircraft we had. We were in a bit of a hurry – hordes of enemy aircraft on their way.'

'So on that occasion he did fly without it. And what happened?'

Charlie paused, considering the question. 'He died.'

Yes, he thought: 'died'; not 'was killed'.

'How terrible, Charlie, truly terrible. I'm sorry. You were close, heh, you and that friend? It's not an easy thing, to lose someone close. But it wasn't your fault, Charlie.'

'No. Not my fault. No one's fault.'

'Just war, Charlie.'

'Just war. War's fault.'

The doctor interrupted. 'I'll take a last look at your arm and head, Charlie, then we leave.'

They walked for a good three or four miles through the darkness, Charlie and the doctor and the farmer, sometimes following this lane or that for a while, sometimes crossing fields, sometimes cutting through tracts of woodland that Charlie suspected were outlying portions of the forest in which he had hidden.

From the position of the thin sliver of moon he decided that they were tacking towards the coast, but very indirectly. The little dog stayed the course with them all the way. The doctor used the flashlight only when they came to obstacles such as fences or ditches.

'You're not armed, you never are, from what I've seen,' said Charlie as the doctor helped him pass beneath a stretch of barbed wire.

'That's not our way,' explained the doctor. 'It's not how we do our fighting. We're an escape line, not an armed movement or guerrillas. Some of our comrades carry arms, I acknowledge that, but only for defence, I hope, not attack. You know I never liked that gun you carry. But of course you must do what's right for you.'

The handover was smoothly effected. They arrived at

a tiny crossroads where four lanes met, surrounded by fields. One of the lanes bridged a dried-up stream. The farmer led Charlie about a hundred yards along the bank, then climbed down and told him to follow. They crouched side by side and waited while the doctor stood at the crossroads, alone but for the dog.

Charlie's nostrils filled with the aromas of the night: of cool grass and, from somewhere, a waft of wild mint. In his pocket he caressed the photograph, more crumpled than ever.

Not long now, he told himself.

A minute later he saw three brief flashes of light followed by a longer flash far across one of the fields. He recognised the Morse: three dots and a dash – V for victory. The doctor responded with his flashlight. Charlie stared into the darkness until his eyes stung. Another couple of minutes passed and at last a man appeared at the crossroads. He and the doctor shook hands and spoke briefly, then the doctor signalled for Charlie to join him.

'I must stay here,' whispered the farmer. 'If anything goes wrong, someone must report back. My turn tonight.'

Charlie took the lump of shrapnel from his pocket and put it into the farmer's hand.

'Give this to your son.'

The farmer chuckled. 'It's that obvious he's mine, heh? He's a good boy.'

'The very best. Be proud.'

'I am. A father should be proud of his son, heh?'

'And a son of his father. I think the doctor is your brother. The woman is your wife.'

159

The farmer chuckled again. 'She was magnificent today. You should have seen her. One day perhaps I'll tell you all about it. Such a woman – I'm very blessed.' He clasped Charlie's hand firmly and shook it. 'Goodbye until then, Charlie.'

Charlie clambered up the bank and went to the crossroads. Down one of the lanes other figures were emerging from the darkness and passing silently into the adjoining field – he saw three figures, then a fourth, one after the other in single file. The man who had greeted the doctor was rejoining them, like a shepherd returning to his flock – a shepherd who carried not a crook but a submachine gun slung over his shoulder.

'You're in good hands, Charlie, the best possible,' whispered the doctor. 'Your escorts are French and Belgian. You'll be told only their code names. Your other companions are probably of several nationalities. Like you, they're on the run – other Allied airmen or soldiers who've been stranded in France or the Low Countries, sometimes for months, or perhaps civilians fleeing arrest and execution or deportation to Germany, which comes to the same thing. It's likely you'll be joined by others along the way. You go south from here and eventually into Spain, that's all I'm permitted to know. You'll be provided with false identity papers – we're not set up to do that here. We're just a tiny tributary flowing into a river that runs all the way through the Netherlands, Belgium and France, a river that's growing as each month passes. Some of your route might be by train but much will be on foot. It won't be easy and it will be dangerous. But soon you'll be in England, Charlie – what you wanted.'

Another firm handshake followed. Charlie bent down and scratched the dog's ears.

'One day this war will be over and our country will be ours again,' added the doctor. 'Come back and see us then.'

'I don't know your names.'

'No, you don't. But you'll find us. Au revoir, Charlie.'

Then the doctor and the little dog retreated into the darkness. The last Charlie saw of them was the small scrap of white, then it too disappeared.

Down the lane, the shepherd with the submachine gun was waiting.

# 25

Henry Banham tossed and turned. Sleep refused to come. He lay on his left side: he grew stiff and uncomfortable. He tried his right side: cramp attacked him. He rolled onto his back: the mattress was filled with rocks.

'Nothing wrong with the bed, dear,' said Rosemary. 'The bed is the same bed as it was last night and all the nights before that, for as long as we've been married. Something's troubling you, that's what. Nothing to do with the bed. You're such a worrier, dear. What is it this time?'

'Nothing, Rosemary, nothing.'

He went downstairs and made tea. As he sipped he recalled his visit to Émilie and what she had told him.

'Charlie is a very driven man, Henry.'

*Sharr-lee*. The way she said it made him smile.

'He certainly is,' he replied. 'And determined. Most stubborn man I know. Never gives up. That's why you mustn't lose hope.'

'Have you ever asked yourself why he's like that?'

'I suppose it's a characteristic I take for granted. All our pilots are driven – though none as much as Charlie.'

'And their reasons are proper and good, Henry – defending their country and loved ones, fighting against evil, reasons like those, normal reasons that people have in this war. Charlie has those too, of course. But he has something else that drives him even more.' She hesitated. 'What do you know about a place in France called Étaples?'

Henry frowned; the question seemed to have nothing to do with what she had been saying. 'What do I know? Well, it's near Le Touquet, there's a big military cemetery of ours there from the last war – Imperial War Graves.' But talk of war dead seemed less than tactful; he cast about for other thoughts. 'We had a field hospital there too – huge place, Germans bombed it several times. I think we had a hospital there this time as well – briefly, until we had to pull out from France.'

He stopped. This was no better. None of it was uplifting. None of it seemed appropriate under the present circumstances.

But Émilie was nodding. 'In the last war it was also a training camp for men on their way to the Western Front, to the trenches – Flanders, Artois, the Somme. Those who had already been through that horror were there too, the wounded, so they knew the reality of war, its terrible truth.

'It was a bad place, Henry, inhuman, not for those reasons but because the people in charge treated the men cruelly, even contemptuously, both the raw recruits and the wounded, who were there only so that they could be sent back to the hell from which they'd come.

'Worst of all, the people in charge had little or no experience of the front. So how could they possibly train others for it or know what the wounded had been through? All the men saw that, of course. Those with real experience saw it most clearly of all and resented it bitterly. You can understand this?'

'I can.'

'To make matters worse, the military police were brutes who abused their power. Many bad things went on. And there were stupid, petty rules such as the town of Le Touquet being reserved for officers. The bridge over the river that leads from Étaples to Le Touquet was even guarded to keep the ordinary men out. But soldiers being soldiers, they found ways – they simply crossed the river, the Canche, at low tide.

'For a time the authorities didn't realise this was happening. Or perhaps they turned a blind eye. But one night some men were found out and arrested as deserters. It was a nonsensical charge, but it carried a death sentence. Their comrades gathered in large numbers to protest. Things went wrong, fighting broke out, shots were even fired. Arrests were made, trials were rushed through and men were sentenced to prison with hard labour. Several were sentenced to death. Some had their sentences commuted but at least one was executed by firing squad.'

She rose to look out of the window to the garden where little Charlie was playing in the sandpit.

'After that, conditions got even tougher. The men became more resentful than ever. Discipline broke down and they mutinied. Reinforcements were brought in and the mutiny was harshly put down. There are different stories about what happened then. Some say only one man was executed as a mutineer, others say more than one. You won't find an official record because the report of the Board of Inquiry was suppressed.' She turned to look at Henry. Her expression was solemn. 'There was a cover-up. Officially the mutiny never happened.' She sighed and sat down. 'What you need to know is that Charlie's father was at that camp, he was in Étaples. That was where he died.'

'Executed? For mutiny?'

'Yes and no.'

'I don't understand.'

'He mutinied, yes. He was arrested. But he escaped. They had to hunt him down. In the end they caught him. He was hiding in woodland. By then the cover-up had begun. So he couldn't be executed for being part of the mutiny – because officially there hadn't been a mutiny.'

'So what happened?'

'He still had to be punished, to be made an example of. He was tried and shot not for mutiny but for cowardice. Charlie's mother had to live with the shame of that – her husband a coward. People reviled her. Worst of all, she didn't know the truth. Her home, Charlie's home, was broken into and everything belonging to her husband was put on a bonfire, even photographs, including their wedding photographs. That's what Charlie grew up with. The only good thing is that some men who knew the truth survived the war, and when they returned home they gave his mother a true account. Charlie also came to know the truth. But even so, he grew up as officially the son of a coward.'

'Which he isn't.'

'No. Henry. He isn't.'

'None of this is on his service record.'

'Of course not. Why would he tell the RAF any of this?'

'He'll come home, Émilie, he'll come back to you. If anyone can do it, Charlie can. Driven and stubborn, that's our Charlie. Best of breed.'

She nodded sadly. 'Yes, Henry.'

Henry finished his tea. He switched off the lamp so that no chink of light would show as he stepped into the back garden, nothing to help a German bomber or alarm a jittery ARP warden.

The night was windless and balmy. A thin crescent of moon was drifting lazily across from France. Such glorious days and sweet nights, this August, as if summer would never end.

He stood there for a long time, looking towards France and thinking about Charlie.

Such a worrier, Henry Banham.

# 26

Despite the hour, Bernard was awake. He had never been asleep.

The shotgun had lain for months concealed in the engine compartment of the same old Berliet delivery van that had sheltered him from the German officer. Now it stood beside his bed, within easy reach. Any time, day or night, when the German next came calling, he would be ready for him.

The septic tank was ready too. Given a few months, only bones and a skull would be left, and bones and skulls had no nationality or military rank. A day's work would see the Kübelwagen cannibalised, stripped down to its last nut and bolt, all dispersed about the yard until needed. The chassis would be left to rot in the lake; other than that, nothing would be wasted.

Nothing except his son's life.


The German officer had been asleep but suddenly started awake.

'Scheisse!'

He hauled himself out of bed and hurriedly began to dress.

Some vague thing had been niggling at him all evening, some uncertain impression, a half thought, a half idea that slipped from his grasp and refused to take form. It was as if a shadow was floating just at the edge of his vision, tantalising him, impossible to ignore, but when he tried to look at it directly, it vanished. So he dismissed it – without even understanding that was what he was doing – and turned to other, more comforting, matters: his health was fine, his consternation over the risk he had taken misplaced; tomorrow he would resume his search for the English pilot and he would be successful this time; and he would find that wretch of a garage owner and deal with him once and for all.

These and other soothing reflections had seen him to bed, and soon he was sleeping soundly.

But then his mind, freed by sleep and through no conscious volition on his part, captured the shadow that had eluded him, pinned it down and defined it clearly.

Oh so clearly.

That hay meadow. Its exhilarating aroma – such relief after the foulness of the garage yard. In the meadow, two men beside a tall rick of hay as he accelerated past. Two men to whom he had paid no heed because he was seeking only one.

A small white dog scampering around their feet. A dog he had seen somewhere before.

But where?

The shadow that had slipped away from him was not this clear and simple question. The shadow was that he had been unable to formulate the question at all, unable to see what he needed to ask.

But now his mind had done his work for him. And with the question no longer at the edge of his vision but right here before him, he knew its answer. He knew where he had seen the dog. The mongrel that he should have shot.

In the darkness he saw the two men again. Saw them well enough to recognise the Destry boy, with that unmistakable nose. But not the other man, the one who was wiping sweat from his face with an old blue cap. Even with that face half hidden, the officer knew he was neither the boy's father nor his uncle. This was a man he had never seen before.

'Scheisse!'

He would go out to the farm tonight. Immediately. Strike while the iron was hot.

Come to think of it, he would go via the garage owner's place. Kill two birds with one stone. Well, kill one and arrest the other.

He would go alone. Always better to work alone. He had learnt that hard lesson.

Yes, these things he would do.


'You're on your way now, Charlie,' said the voice.

Charlie found himself staring into the darkness again. The stranger was there, barely visible, this forgettable sort of man who moved in shadows and in silence, who came and went without warning like a wisp of river mist.

And who was no stranger at all.

'You don't need my help any more, Charlie. You'll be fine now.'

'Tell me your name.'

'You said my name didn't matter.'

'I've changed my mind. I know it anyway, but tell me.'

'Same as yours, Charlie. My name is Charlie. Family tradition.'

Then he melted back into the night.


Was the noise real or was it in her dream?

Émilie was not sure. In the dream she was with Charlie. They were on a beach, in warm sunshine. Glittering sand was trickling through his fingers.

'Marry me,' he was saying.

So painful to wake from such a dream on this loneliest of nights.

She went downstairs, quietly. The front door was locked. The back door too.

She went through to the living room. She glanced at the window to make sure the curtains were closed and the blackout blind was in place, then switched on the light.

At once her gaze fell on what was in the middle of the room.

Directly in front of the fireplace, on the rug, was a small cone of sand like a tiny pyramid. She knelt down beside it, scooped up a handful of the sand and let it trickle through her fingers.

'Oh Charlie,' she whispered.

# VILLA NORMANDIE

May 1944. The Normandy coastal village of Caillons is under German occupation, its villagers struggling to survive. With her husband forced into compulsory service for the German Reich, Jeanne Dupré, mother of two adolescent daughters, risks everything to lead the local French Resistance cell.

Life becomes even more dangerous with the arrival of British agent Daniel Benedict. He needs Jeanne's help to complete his mission, vital to Operation Overlord, the D-Day landings. Jeanne is suspicious that Benedict and she are not fighting for the same outcome.

Their joint foe is Jürgen Graf, Nazi oberleutnant set on wiping out the local Resistance. Aware that a spy is at large, Graf is on a ruthless mission to hunt Benedict down.

With the help of a network of Catholic priests, Benedict penetrates the heart of the Nazis' defences against Allied invasion, the Atlantic Wall.

As the lives of Jeanne and Benedict become increasingly intertwined, can they stay true to themselves? Will they have to sacrifice all in their fight for freedom?

*Villa Normandie* is a moving historical novel, presenting an accurate picture of life under Nazi occupation. It is thoroughly detailed, meticulously researched and vividly authentic, depicting the turbulent world of the French Resistance and the struggle of the French people for freedom.

ALSO BY KEVIN DOHERTY

# PATRIOTS

Russia. The 1980s. The Cold War is still raging.

Mikhail Gorbachev's strict vision for Russia is driving out the economic corruption that riddled the old Soviet regime.

Nikolai Serov watches as traitors in positions of the highest authority are forced into revealing their hands, knowing that he does not want to fall victim to the same fate of arrest and execution.

As head of the KGB's First Chief Directorate and one of Moscow's leading black marketeers and drug kings, Serov recognises that he has only one chance to construct a sophisticated plot that will ensure his own freedom.

Serov's intricate plan unfolds in a calculated web of murder and betrayal as he activates a Russian mole who has lain dormant for the past twenty years and now is at the top rung of Britain's MI5.

His vision for the future stretches far and wide as his secret master plan succeeds in influencing East and West policy and dictates the fates of governments on both sides.

*Patriots* takes the reader right to the heart of Cold War Russia. Meticulously researched, complexly plotted, explosively violent and ruthlessly authentic, it is the first novel to deal with the darker side of Gorbachev's programmes of perestroika and glasnost.

*Patriots* is a gripping tale of power politics and treachery at the highest levels of government and the intelligence services.

Printed in Great Britain
by Amazon